THE OFFING

THE OFFING

BENJAMIN MYERS

BLOOMSBURY PUBLISHING
LONDON • OXFORD • NEW YORK • NEW DELHI • SYDNEY

BLOOMSBURY PUBLISHING
Bloomsbury Publishing Plc
50 Bedford Square, London, WC1B 3DP, UK

BLOOMSBURY, BLOOMSBURY PUBLISHING and the Diana logo are trademarks
of Bloomsbury Publishing Plc

First published in Great Britain, 2019

A catalogue record for this book is available from the British Library

ISBN: HB: 978-1-5266-1131-4; TPB: 978-1-5266-1129-1; EBOOK: 978-1-5266-1127-7

2 4 6 8 10 9 7 5 3 1

Typeset by Integra Software Services Pvt. Ltd
Printed and bound in Great Britain by CPI Group (UK) Ltd, Croydon CRO 4YY

To find out more about our authors and books visit www.bloomsbury.com
and sign up for our newsletters

For Adelle

I've left my own old home of homes,
Green fields and every pleasant place;
The summer like a stranger comes,
I pause and hardly know her face.

'The Flitting', John Clare

Where did life go?

Every day I find myself asking this one same question of the mirror, yet the answer always eludes me. All I see is a stranger staring back.

So I shuffle to the kitchen, where I stir my tea and spoon my morning oats and mutter the mantra – you'll never be as young as you are right now – but it feels hollow between my lips. I cannot trick time, nor myself. I'll always be as old as I am right now, then older.

The paint on the floorboards has been worn away by the drag of my feet, which ache from walking a million miles, and the wooden lengths are warped now like the hull of a landed galleon, and the meadow is wild too as the days slip away and the seasons shorten. A few summers here, some long dark winters there; good fortune, infamy, illness, a little love, a little more luck and suddenly you're looking down the wrong end of the telescope.

Everything aches these days, not just the feet. My legs, my hands, my eyes. My wrists and fingers throb from a lifetime of hammering the keyboards. A constant pain nags at my neck and I marvel at the minor miracle that my body has held out this long. Sometimes it feels as if it is held together by little other than strings of memories and sinews of hope. The mind is a museum coated in dust.

But I was a young man once, so young and green, and that can never change. Memory allows me to be so again.

I knew not what language could do then. I did not yet understand the power and potency of words. The complex magic of language was as alien as the altered country that I saw around me during that summer. Something insidious grows within me now; its roots are deeply anchored. Vines reach around corners to clutch and tighten. I am a passive host. Too tired to fight, I accept it and instead sit back and merely wonder where life went. And I wait.

My desk is old and the chair creaks. Twice I have had the joints fixed and the upholstery replaced. Every so often the old wood-burning stove coughs smoke back into the room, and the guttering is clogged with moss. One window is cracked and soon I will need to find someone to fix the roof. The whole place needs a lot of work but I am too ancient for all that now; the building and its contents will outlast me. The old word processor still functions, though. There's power in the both of us, there is electricity, and while it is still there I have something to share.

Sitting here now by the open window, a glissando of birdsong on the very lightest of breezes that carries with it the scent of a final incoming summer, I cling to poetry as I cling to life.

I

The bay opened out before me, a great glacial basin carved by creaking ice and trickling water hundreds of thousands of years ago.

I approached it from the north and saw a giant semi-amphitheatre that held within it farms and hamlets as the land funnelled downwards from the purpling moors, and below them the fields ran all the way to an opaline sea, over which there perilously perched a huddled cluster of houses jiggered together in a cleft in the land. Between them and the water, a narrow sweep of glittering sand. A bronze band.

The houses sat haphazardly above the ebbing tide on a crumbling cliff face of loose soil and wet clay that was slowly being eroded by the salt spray and circling fret. The homes resembled stranded sailors shipwrecked by the storms of centuries. Time itself was chipping away at this coastal reach, sculpting the island anew in an age of uncertainty.

I thought about how the sea served to remind of the finite existence of solid matter, and that the only true boundaries are not trenches and shelters and checkpoints but those between rock and sea and sky.

Here I stopped to refill my flask from a roadside spring that fed into a stone trough, feeling as if I had wandered into a painting. The sun was a brilliant bright disc of shimmering white over a scumbled scape and I understood, perhaps for the first time, what it was that made men wish to pick up a paintbrush or compose a verse: an impulse to capture the pulse-quickening sensation, this *nowness* evoked by a vista as breathtaking as it was unexpected. Art was an attempt to preserve the amber of the moment.

The fresh water slipped down my throat like cords of silk, cooling my stomach for a moment, and pooling there. Water never tastes finer than that drawn fresh from the ground and drunk from metal; whether receptacle, ladle or spout, it seems somehow to bring the flavour alive.

I drank more and then cupped my hands and held them there, a dub in the pinkness of my palms, then patted the water onto my forehead, face and neck. I filled my flask again and walked on.

———

There had been a war and though the conflict was over it still raged on in those men and women who had brought it home with them.

6

It was kept alive in their eyes or hung heavy about their shoulders like a blood-soaked cloak. It blossomed too in their hearts, a black flower that had taken root there, never to be eradicated. The seeds were too toxic, too deeply sown, for the memories to be anything but perennially poisonous.

Wars continue long after the fighting has stopped, and the world felt then as if it were full of holes. It appeared to me scarred and shattered, a place made senseless by those in positions of power. Everything was fragments, everything burnt.

I was neither old enough to have made myself a hero nor young enough to have escaped the newsreel images or the long dark shadows that the returning soldiers dragged behind them like empty coffins. For no one ever really wins a war: some just lose a little less than others.

I was a child when it began and a young man when it ended and in the wake of this conflict visible loss was everywhere, hanging like a great heavy cloud over the island, and no amount of red, white and blue bunting or medals pinned to the sobbing chests of its survivors could change that.

The history books should not entirely be believed: Allied victory did not taste sweet and the winters that followed would be as frosted and unforgiving as any. Because although the elements care little for the madness of men, even the white virginal snow would now appear impure to those who had seen the first footage of barbed wire and body pits.

Yet viewed through the eyes of the young the conflict was an abstraction, a memory once removed and already fading. It wasn't *our* war. It wouldn't ruin *our* lives before they had even started.

On the contrary, it had awakened within me a sense of adventure, a wanderlust to step beyond the end of the street where the flagstones finally gave themselves to the fields, and industrial Northern England stretched away beneath the first warm haze of a coming season of growth, to explore whatever it was that lay beyond this shimmering mirage that turned the horizon into an undulating ocean of blossoming greens.

I was sixteen and free, and hungry. Hungry for food, as we all were – the shortage continued for many years – yet my appetite was for more than the merely edible. To those blessed with the gift of living, it seemed as if the present moment was a precious empty vessel waiting to be filled with experience. Time was more valuable now; it was the only thing we had in abundance, though war had taught us that this too was a limited resource, and to spend it unwisely or wastefully was as great a sin as any.

Young men and women we were, and it was for those fellows who had fallen in foreign fields, or been shot down from skies like grouse on the Glorious Twelfth, or those poor withered souls interred in the mass graves, that we were living now.

Life was out there, ready and waiting to be eaten in greedy gulps. To be scoffed and swallowed. My sensations were awakened, and insatiable, and I owed it to myself, and to all those like me who had died screaming for their mothers or drowning in thickening pools of themselves, to gorge myself.

More than anything, though, was the allure of a natural world in which I intended to immerse myself. I knew from books that the North offered a diverse terrain of wolds and woods, moors and fells, dales and valleys, all inhabited by plant and animal species waiting to be seen by my wide and wandering eye.

At home I had exhausted the possibilities. I had diligently recorded all sightings of passing birds, migratory or otherwise. I had built a small collection of bones and skulls, carefully debrided and scrubbed clean of flesh, and kept in a tea chest by the concrete coal bunker beyond the back door as my mother would not allow them in the house. I had fished and ferreted, ratted and ensnared, and on one guilty occasion even removed the egg of a sitting raven from its crag-top eyrie, though had soon grown ill at the thought of animals killed for sport, hunted for the thrill. Even to disturb their patterns felt sinful. So much adolescent time had been spent up trees, yet I was tired of the same views now, the same predictable seasonal changes. I wanted to experience so much more of what was happening out there, beyond the confines of the rural colliery village that sat in the softly undulating fields, somewhere between the city and the sea. I wanted to be surprised. Only when alone in the wild had I ever come remotely close to beginning to know my true self; the rest of the time was mere playground noise and classroom instruction, domestic duty and banal distraction.

———

I had set out in spring, impatient, a pack on my back containing the bare essentials for a journey whose only aim was transience: a sleeping bag, a blanket and groundsheet, a change of clothes. Two camping pans, a cup, my flask, penknife, fork, spoon and plate. A trowel for outdoor business. No map.

I had no need for a razor either.

I also carried with me a notepad and pen, a bar of soap, a toothbrush and matches, and a Jew's harp gifted to me by my grandfather, who offered the sage advice that if one could master a musical instrument one could always make money, for the English were a nation who valued effort over talent and thought that *having a go* was enough, and though I had not yet taught myself to play this strange and haunted-sounding instrument, I certainly intended to. Ahead of me down the tracks and lanes I envisaged plenty of free time, and a fair few nights whose lonely silence would surely benefit from some music, however discordant and ineptly delivered it might be.

On the morning of my departure my mam also insisted on squeezing into my bag a pack-up containing some thick slices of ham, cheese, apples and a large stottie, all wrapped in a facecloth that she made me promise upon God's good name that I would use at least once a day.

There was still a nip in the air when I left the ancient city, joining the river below the high turrets of the great cathedral, looming loftily from its natural promontory. I let the slow-moving waterway guide me as I followed it upstream through a wooded gorge, then beyond that out into the great unknown.

The larger part of my young years so far had been spent staring out of classroom windows longing for a life lived outside, willing the bell to chime down the corridors so that I might run free through the fields.

And now here, finally, it was all around me, an unfolding wonderland, a swirling season in bloom alive with the warm sound of wood pigeons and drilling woodpeckers, and the scents of ragwort, balsam and, beyond the trees in the sloping fields, the heady, sedative musk of rapeseed.

Soon too there would be the sight of swallows and swifts returning from North Africa to summer here, the centre of the world, Northern England, the greenest land there ever was, so pungent and lush it could make a young man dizzy.

Along the riverbanks wild garlic grew, peppering the air. As I walked I plucked the leathery leaves and chewed them, the rich, raw taste viscous on my tongue. Oily almost.

I left the Wear as I knew that if I continued it would take me west, to the upland dales of Wolsingham,

Westgate and Wearhead, where they said the river bubbled up from the soil, little more than a gurgling belch of a thing, and beyond it nothing but tiny villages with names like Cowshill and Cornriggs. Employment would be scant there.

Here and there I walked on tracks and alongside warm bitumen roads. I came across abandoned quarries, wide chasms in the earth, open and ragged like gaping tooth extractions. I picked my way through the rusting remains of wagon rails and tin- and slate-mine trails. I passed closed-down gypsum works and clearings containing cable spools and tipped dolly carts, but no other signs of man. Whenever possible I kept to the woods and glades, fields and dales.

I found work where I went, at farms and on smallholdings. Piecework mainly, and odd jobs at solitary houses, as many families had lost men, or had seen them return depleted, decrepit or broken, parts of them missing like second-hand jigsaw puzzles. Few had returned fully fit and functional enough to resume their lives as if nothing had changed, and though many were still strong of body, they were now no longer muscular of mind.

These homes always needed young brawn to do the tasks that these broken-toy men could no longer complete and few doors I knocked on turned me away. Behind them I found quiet survivors who had seen things previously unimaginable. War was an illness in a way, treatable only by the passing of time, and many were stricken until the end of their days.

I steadily laboured across to where Durham met Cumbria and Cumbria shook hands with North Yorkshire, where the mining of tin and lead were still the local industries, or else the farming of sheep took place on the windswept slopes of the upper moors all year round, the woolly-backed creatures corralled and clipped in the summer and dug out of drifts in the long, lingering winters. It was a different landscape to the one I was accustomed to – it was also sculpted and scarred but in a somehow more agreeable way. The newness of the unfamiliar was intoxicating. It even sounded different here, the empty vastness of the moors a whispering place free of the clang and clatter of colliery life. A place weighted with myth. It was thrilling.

At one such farm I kissed a taciturn girl called Theresa who tasted of aniseed, and whose curious sugary tongue probed my mouth for a full ten seconds before she turned and ran away without a word, and though she explored me with a vigour that bordered on the violent, her disinterest so equally sudden that I might as well have been a passing donkey, I was still aware I had passed a small milestone in my life. No one back at home would ever believe me, of course, the gymnasium changing room already busy with tall stories of unseen girls kissed in faraway places. These things only ever happened elsewhere, without witness. And now I actually was in the kingdom of elsewhere, free from the shackles of familiarity of place and people.

The soil was bad for growing in the Dales and the houses too far apart, so I headed south, logging and lambing, droving and driving, chopping and chipping. A day here, a day there, following the sun and resting when it was time to rest. For once I was not a slave to the leaden ticking of the classroom clock, whose hands appeared on certain days to move with torturously slow delight, and once or twice even seemed to stop entirely, the frozen moment stretching into an aeon as all around me my classmates were oblivious to this conspiracy to hold us trapped and captive forever. Instead I became my own master and at each turned corner slithered further free from my adolescent skin.

When exhaustion came upon me I bedded down in barns and sheds and caravans long abandoned, and on several occasions slept the sleep of the dead wedged tight beneath hedgerow walls of bramble and holly, planted perhaps in medieval times, ten feet tall and as impenetrable as rolls of Bergen-Belsen barbed wire.

On other nights, when the sky was clear of clouds and the farmers predicted a dry patch, I found open fields and pitched my sheet into a tent shape to sleep with the glow of a dying fire upon my moon-turned face, a bed of flattened grass beneath my back, awakening stiff and often bone-soaked, cursing the farmers' useless predictions.

Food was gifted. I existed mainly on eggs and potatoes and last autumn's apples, and would on occasion
be given milk for my flask or some fresh balls of butter
wrapped in a hessian twist, and perhaps the heel end of
a loaf so dry it could have been fired at the brickworks. I
was given greens too. Spinach and chard were in season.
Sometimes a turnip, chunks of which I chewed raw,
but never took to. Meat was scarce. Once I received
a jar of honey, into which I found I could dip almost
anything. Even a cube of turnip speared on my fork-
end became an edible delicacy if I shut my eyes and
crunched through to its bitter centre.

As the distance from everything I had ever known
increased I began to feel a sense of lightness about
myself. The anxiety that had sat sour in the pit of my
stomach during the final year of school began to abate,
and with that came a sense of mental clarity. For the
first time I was out of the shadows of the creaking,
clanking mine-head and away from the dark-grey dust
that on still, clear days seemed to settle everywhere and
had to be beaten out of bed sheets and drying linen
on clothes lines strung across the back alleys. Now I
breathed deeply and felt a spring in my stride that on
the brightening mornings made me believe I could
traipse for days without stopping. I also felt my bones,
joints, muscles and mind working together in perfect

symbiosis like the parts of a well-oiled machine fuelled by little more than youth and just enough food.

For as long as I had been able to listen, the inevitability of a lifelong career down in the dusty darkness had lurked like a spectre stalking the subconscious, casting a pall over everything. I had first feared the thought but more recently had grown to hate it to the point of stubborn dissension.

My parents had never even entertained the idea that I might do anything else but join the pit. There were boys I had grown up with who had already done two or three years at the coalface, yet for one so infatuated with fresh air and solitude, the expectation that I would follow my father down the shafts as he had his father before him was the very reason I was walking the lanes of England now. It was an act of escapology and rebellion, yet the ties of the community were still pulled tight enough to make me wonder whether this was merely a short-term reprieve, a first and last hurrah before the dire prospect of *knuckling down*. I had to at least try to see another world before coal – or, worse, war – took me over entirely.

Spring revealed itself around me. Many characters I met on the way in those warming weeks: tramps and trawlermen and several travellers of the road. Tinkers or tatters, they were called, who made their money patching up pots and pans, cutting and weaving willows, buying and selling. I once shared a fire with a family of seven who each night somehow crammed themselves into a bow-top vardo towed by a gentle old cob.

The war's aftermath was still proving to be kind to those who had skills in the arts of thriftiness and bricolage, though. I encountered land-bound sailors in no hurry to take to the sea again, fruit pickers anxiously awaiting the first flourish of bilberries or blackberries, hops pickers biding their time before heading south for full summer, and men who slapped the roads with huge brushes hoisted from great smoking vats of tarmac; I passed idle minutes with the lost and the shell-shocked, survivors one and all.

The weather was the key to unlock these conversations with strangers, the English being a nation obsessed with it being too hot or too cold, or too wet, or just not wet enough. Rare it is to hear an Englishman remark upon the perfection of the meteorological conditions or the greenness of his grass, when he knows it is greener a county over. Weather talk is but a veiled code or a currency to exchange, a transaction as a means to moving things along to something more considered once reciprocal trust has been won. This I learned along the way, as circumstance and the practicalities of survival forced me to open my mouth more often than I was used to at home, where most of my interactions with adults simply involved obeying their orders via a series of bovine grunts and anatine honks. An initial sense of loneliness first loosened my tongue, though I soon learned that solitude in the wild was not to be feared; in fact, I experienced frequent and quite unexpected moments of exhilaration at the overwhelming sense of purposelessness that I now had. I go could anywhere, do anything. Be anyone.

During these dialogues with strangers the war was barely mentioned; that beast stayed buried. It did not bear exhumation.

———

In time I tired of the ditches and copses, and felt instead the lure of the sea, so I turned towards Europe, following the road signs that led down through villages that clung to Cleveland and North Yorkshire's eastern edge.

Skinningrove and Loftus.

Staithes and Hinderwell.

In each I found enough work to sustain me for a day or two before moving on.

I went to Runswick Bay, Sandsend and then finally entered the town of Whitby with its whalebone archway and vinegar breeze, and across the bay I saw the skeleton of an old abbey perched in silhouette.

Twice along this stretch of coast I passed planes that had been shot down from skies split by conflict, one a blackened abstraction of flame-twisted metal, its glass melted away in a howling fireball. The second I found sitting in a cornfield with one wing missing, but otherwise intact, its nose coming to rest in the fledgling wheat heads that grew around it now as if it had been idly parked there by picnicking day-trippers.

Yet there on the tail and the remaining wing were the pernicious insignias of an empire of horror, and scattered around it the debris of death's grim mission, not yet removed by local lads who had somehow missed this bounty: a contorted propeller blade as long as I was tall and a ragged piece of cloth that I did not dare to pick up. It felt as if the bomber had only come down minutes earlier in a spiralling descent over the irregular chequerboard fields of a foreign land, smoke trailing, death rising up to greet its hurriedly praying pilot, one more victim in the mad folly-dance of conflict. Another ghosted statistic.

I did not linger here, and soon I peaked the hill of High Normanby and looked down across the grazing slopes of Fylingthorpe, and below it the bay, its waters a beautiful mosaic made from a shattered mirror of emerald and malachite.

II

As I passed through fields that ran to the sea, rust-coloured pollen clung to my trousers and created a pattern of motes, and when I brushed it with a thumb it streaked a smudge the colour of coralline, of a slow-setting sun.

The houses I saw were stout and strong and built from pale Goathland stone. Moor-quarried, weather-worn and red-tiled, they were attractive dwellings, many set in their own patches of land, and quite unlike the soot-streaked houses squashed together into terraces in the tight-bricked villages of home.

This was agricultural rather than industrial terrain – of the earth rather than stained by it.

Hedges hemmed me in and I passed herds of cows with udders dangling like party balloons from last Christmas and the occasional horse too, tethered in lacklustre paddocks, ribs showing like the hulls of beached old boats, wide wet eyes searching the ground for something more than stubble. War's grim legacy had not spared the animals, but so long as their hearts were beating there was hope for these half-starved creatures yet.

There were also sheep scattered about the hillsides, and in one field was what appeared to be an absurd distortion of a sheep – a strange beast the size of a small horse, with an elongated neck and wool-covered legs, which I would later learn was an alpaca.

Walking downhill into the gentle breeze that was blowing in from the sea provided sweet relief. The smell of a seasonal shifting was in the air: a fresh green sharpness of wild grasses, juice-filled shoots and rising sap that scented the winding lanes, the hedgerows creating the impression of being in a maze as I chose forks at will and let the great slopes take me.

My soundtrack was the bleating March-born lambs, now sheep, soon to be shorn. Life was here, it was happening all around me, and in me, and through me in this new season of great growth and beautiful birth, this time of violent teeming.

Down winding lanes I walked, the sea almost mirage-like in the mind of a young man whose only maritime experience had been a yawning childhood morning spent watching the choppy grey waters slapping at the stone docks of the shipyards of Sunderland.

Even then my first impression of the sea had not been of the water itself, but that which fed off it and into it: a world of rivets and sparks, of fire and noise, and great grey monstrous structures like steel cathedrals stripped down and tipped sideways, hulking half-finished warships whose brute dimensions were almost beyond comprehension.

The whisper of the waves had been drowned out by the screech of metal on metal, and the screech of the seagulls suspended high above.

I remembered nothing of the water itself, only that it had skulked beyond, barely seen, behind the concrete of a dry dock and the shipyard's metal fencing containing man's industrious cacophony.

My father had taken me there on a rare day off; fifteen miles and two long hours by a bus whose upper deck swirled thick with the blue smoke of Players and Capstans. We had pulled crabs from the drab water of the harbour using thick string lines weighted by six-inch nails and baited with fatty knuckles of ham saved from the butcher's drain. The smell of petroleum and the crabs' luminescent green shells had been enough to put us off eating them, and we'd tipped the bucketful back into the unctuous water.

Yet here, only sixty or seventy miles further south, down a coast which I had wandered for many weeks, the shipyards and the coke-blackened waters of Wearmouth were far behind me. The land flowed forward now in a grassy tessellation of fields farmed and grazed, and divided by dusty tracks and densely packed tree-covered glades. Through these shaded, sunken fissures ran tiny arterial waterways, as clear as glass and singing sweetly on their way to meet the lambent salt water of a North

Sea that sparkled as if its surface were made entirely from a million-strong shoal of freshly spawned herring.

There was a different coastal purpose here than in the dry docks and dumping wagons of home, where the sea served as production line to an industry that had profited from war, and the tired tides chipped away at the shortening cliff line with the dull repetition of a mason's mallet.

Here the ocean was a gateway, an open invitation, and I accepted it readily.

———

I followed trails through whispering meadows and rutted thickets, vaulting stone walls, climbing stiles and passing through kissing gates whose top rungs were worn skull-smooth by the clammy palms of several centuries of passing land workers and hill wanderers.

I took an even narrower lane that was not built for vehicles, then at a bend in the way the track dipped into a wooded pass and here I crossed a shallow ford by ancient stepping stones where time was once again imprinted by the hollowed curves of hobnailed feet on cold hewn rock. I couldn't help but wonder if these stones would still be standing in another hundred years' time, or whether the stream would be poisoned, the old cottages wrecked, the pastures overgrown like neglected cemeteries. Would, I wondered, another war consume it all?

I was following an ancient network of paths, each a winding groove carved into the arid brickearth, a notching of time.

Deep down in the cool dark throat of one such subterranean route I saw a badger sett burrowed into the dirt bankside and surrounded by mounded heaps of impacted soil. Dry, they rose to six or seven feet in height in places. These sculpted slopes led into winding chambers embellished with freshly scratched claw marks. Here were hieroglyphics, a wordless poetry of sorts, and close by clear patterns of tunnelling runs led away through hedge gaps and into the long grass of the surrounding pastures. The vast sett's passages must have run for forty or fifty feet in any direction, pressing deep into the tenebrous domain that had been colonised by this enigmatic animal for generations. They were portals to the kingdom of these fascinating creatures.

As the sun shone down in a series of shafts to the dry pressed earth and highlighted the claw-mark calligraphy, I paused for a moment, aware that I was more than likely close to a family, asleep down in their earthen bunkers, the outside world muted.

I took a swig from my flask but found it empty.

I noted the location, then crawled beneath a fence to cross an open field, trudging shin-deep in waxy grass, through which the incoming sea breeze gently whistled. Guided only by gravity's pull of the downhill camber, I soon met another track, and then turned left off it.

Something drew me down that lane even though it had the appearance of leading to a dead end. This was to become one of those moments when life presents a new path whose importance may only be fully understood in years to come.

A hundred yards on, the lane narrowed and I came upon a cottage butting up against what had now turned into a rough track pitted with ruts and gouged-out ankle-turning hollows.

The house was built of local stone and was covered by a Virginia creeper that clung to it like an octopus to a rock in a storm, its tangled vines reaching tentacle-like around corners. I came upon the house from the rear and traced the strangulating plant's root as it rose from the ground to run around the side of the building, its leaves fluttering in succession when a light breeze ran across it.

It appeared as if in a dream.

The lane ended at the side of the cottage, beyond which was nothing but a jungle of scrubland. In front of the house I could see a garden that held a small terrace of cracked paving stones, a lawn and a vegetable patch trimmed with herbaceous borders, all contained by a crooked wooden fence whose bubbled white paintwork had been blistered, chipped and sanded away by the salty air.

The garden was a small semi-colonised corner of a wild downhill-sloping meadow that directed the eye to the sea a mile or so away, hedges and trees on either side framing it in the manner of a Romantic painter's viewfinder.

Several bird tables were busy with a variety of tits and finches, robins, chiffchaffs and blackcaps, and I watched them for a moment, silent and unseen, until three circling crows descended, their shadows crossing the sun before they dispersed the feast with mercenary efficiency, and I noticed then that crafted beneath the overhanging eaves of a red-brick outbuilding that adjoined the house were two nests of clay and feather, the homes of wrens in residence, shaped like thrown bowls fresh from a potter's wheel.

It was then that I heard a snarling; a low growl like an engine turning over. The sound of phlegm and flesh. Throaty.

I looked over my shoulder to see a large German shepherd poised like a sprinter awaiting the starter's gun, its alert ears pinned back and tail pointed like a wireless antenna. His seeking eyes were fixed on the prize: my wrist. I did not move.

This brutish-looking hound stared, the wet flesh of his top lip peeling back to show his elongated incisors and the brilliant pink-and-black marbling of his gums and palate. He growled again, a low curdle. Meaty thunder.

'Butters,' said a voice as a woman straightened to full length from the thick meadow scrub beyond the garden fence. She turned towards the dog, and then to me. 'Oh, there you are.'

The familiarity of her greeting, spoken as if I had just popped away to boil a pan of water, or twist some carrots from the ground, caught me off guard. I assumed either her eyesight was failing, and she had mistaken me for someone else, or that she was talking directly to the dog. Perhaps she hadn't even seen me at all and any moment now her husband or son – a muscular countryman with arms like hams and an unhealthy suspicion of uninvited strangers – would emerge from an unseen potting shed to take out all his prejudices against hedge-mumpers and ditch-dwellers like me, a slight wandering lad from the ash-coloured coalfields.

The lady was tall, edging six feet, her posture defiant and unapologetic, proud, which only made her appear taller, and stately too.

Her face was angular and catlike, her cheekbones defined and her jaw strong. Her mouth appeared wide – almost too wide for her face – and also feline in its slight upturning at the edges. It suggested a smile suppressed.

I could not accurately have guessed at her age for the young always judge anyone over forty to be old, but I could see the earlier version of her within immediately. It was there in her eyes, and in her movements too. Though her clothes seemed impossibly out of place – Victorian, perhaps – there was a lightness to the way she moved towards me, her gait nimble and seemingly untroubled by either the weight of ageing or the threat of a sweating stranger.

'Get by, Butters,' she said, and at this the dog lowered himself to the ground and rested his head on his paws, but with his eyes still trained on me. 'He's all mouth and no trousers,' she continued. 'He just likes to greet visitors in his own way.'

I found my tongue fumbling for a response, but whatever it was I attempted to say came out as a dry, surprised croak. A parched rasp.

'I call him Butler, for obvious reasons,' she continued. 'Butters for short – though of course "Butters" is, in fact, a longer word.'

My thirst suddenly apparent, I swallowed and tried to summon saliva to lubricate the words that would not come. 'I just came down the lane,' I said by way of a clumsy explanation.

'Yes, I expect you did,' she said. 'You would have had to – and from somewhere far beyond it, judging by your accent, which, if I'm not mistaken, has something of the pitmatic twang about it?'

I did not then know that 'pitmatic' was the name given to the dialect of those who lived in the colliery villages of the North-East, nor that I even had an accent at all. As I tried to speak, though, I was aware that all of a sudden my tongue felt thick in my mouth. It was errant, and the muscles around my mouth felt beyond my control too. Nothing came.

'Well, anyway,' she continued, 'you're just in time for tea. Will you have some?'

I managed to muster a reply. 'Tea?'

'Yes. A cup of. If not more.'

If my accent was that of an outsider, then this lady's was not one I was used to hearing either, and more like that of someone you might only ever hear on the wireless. It was a far cry from the clipped sing-song dialect of the coalfields I grew up hearing.

'If it's not any trouble.'

She shrugged. 'It's no trouble for me so long as you fetch the nettles.'

'Nettles?'

'Yes,' she said. 'We're having nettle tea. Do you take it?'

I hesitated, then shook my head. 'I always thought nettles were poisonous.'

'Poisonous? Of course not. They might *sting*, but that comes only from the tiny hairs on the leaves and stems, which act like tiny needles. When boiled they soon become ineffective.' She paused. 'Your reticence is to be expected. Folklore has taught us to fear this weed; to me it is a friend. It began out of necessity, this nettle habit of mine, but I've found it's as good a quencher as any, and you look like you're spitting feathers.'

'I am rather thirsty, missus.'

'Well, then. But you're not to call me "missus" if you're going to linger.' The woman stepped towards me and extended a gloved hand. 'If you must call me anything, call me by my name: Dulcie. Dulcie Piper. This earthy formality is endearing but it's not necessary.'

After weeks of rough sleeping, I was suddenly aware of my appearance, which despite following my mother's wishes was surely shabby. But if she noticed, Dulcie didn't remark upon it.

'Right,' I said, my face flushed.

'Now is when you tell me your name.'

I forced an awkward smile and took her hand. The gardening glove felt as dry and coarse as my throat. 'It's Robert, miss—'

At this she tutted and wagged a long finger. 'And what's your family name, Robert?'

'It's Appleyard.'

'Well, now. Listen, Robert, while I explain the simple procedure for the perfect brew of nettles. Simply take a generous fistful of this poor old *Urtica dioica*, the most maligned of all the indigenous weeds, and boil it in a pot of aqua vitae – and there is no water purer than that which gurgles up through the Yorkshire strata – then once mashed add either three squeezes or one thick slice of lemon until the tea turns a peony-pink in colour. Serve in a tin mess cup or fine Ming china, for it matters not.'

Embarrassment prevented me from admitting that I had neither seen nor tasted a lemon, and didn't fully understand what she was on about, but perhaps recognising this the old woman spared me further explanation.

'I know what you're thinking: how does one acquire lemons in a land bereft? Let's just say I have contacts. *Connections.* That impotent little Hun has destroyed many things but not this girl's tea habit. No. There are alternatives to lemon too. Thyme, basil, myrtle and verbena could all be seen to replicate the flavour

31

in some way, and of course there is lemon balm and lemongrass – though, unless you're a botanist hotfooting across the continents, I very much doubt you would be able to get your hands on those any time soon. As for limes: forget it. They're as rare as Hitler's left gland if the playground songs are to be believed. Even *I* can't get my hands on them. Limes, I mean.'

Wrong-footed by the scattergun thought process of this curious woman, I missed the joke entirely. 'Why lemon?' I asked cautiously.

'Well, for colour and flavour. One needs a little colour in life, even if it is illusory. And life without flavour is death. Nettle tea is a rather dull drink made tolerable by lemon. One thing in its favour: you don't need a coupon to purchase it. You just help yourself. The leaves are entirely free and anything free always tastes better. Wouldn't you agree?'

'I would,' I said, nodding. 'Yes, I would indeed. I've been living off the land myself a little of late.'

'And good for you. They say it's a panacea too, nettle tea. A boon for your skin, a tonic for your joints and an alarm clock for your movements. At my age you take all the help you can get. It eases the burden upon the meadow too, yanking it up.'

As she walked past me towards the house, the dog raised his head and the way in which he slowly unfolded his legs and rose to full height reminded me of the clothes horse on which my mother hung the starched household whites.

'Don't you get stung?' I asked. 'Picking it, I mean.'

She walked into the house and then appeared a moment later. 'Not if you have the right technique. Use a finger and thumb to grasp the leaf with confidence and you'll be alright. It's the tentative pluckers that come off worst but the thing you *really* have to watch out for are the low-growing ones, for they'll pepper your shins with welts given half a chance and then itch all night long. Worse things have happened at sea, but seeing as you don't yet have the technique – '

She took off the well-worn pair of gardening gloves and tossed them to me. 'Try these. I'll get the water on.'

I slipped on the gloves and felt a clammy warmth from this odd old lady's palms that reminded me of cricket games on the rec back at home, and the one shared pair of batsman's gloves, passed from boy to boy until they were nothing but threadbare shells of stale sweat and tattered rubber.

Dulcie returned carrying a tea tray that she placed on the table, and then she poured the steaming pink drink into cups. 'I had a few leaves left over from the last batch,' she said.

There was a plate of raisin biscuits too that she offered to me. I placed the gloves on the table and took one. I held it in my hand and turned it for a long moment, savouring its appearance as tiny sugar crystals seemed to hold within them the light of the sun, before taking a small and tentative bite.

'Now then,' she said, blowing on her cup. 'A pot of tea for your story seems a fair trade. On your way down bay, are you?'

'Yes, I think so.'

'You don't seem certain.'

'No.'

I didn't elaborate. I took a sip of tea and had my first ever taste of lemon: stringent but not unpleasant. I drank some more.

'We live in a most shadowed present,' said Dulcie. 'These are uncertain times.'

'I just decided to go for a wander. That was a few weeks back.'

She laughed into her tea at this, and a bit slopped out of her cup. 'Oh, I like that. *That* shows spirit.'

We drank our tea looking out into the meadow beyond. I got a better look at the garden, a small area in otherwise wild surroundings, the meadow encroaching on this landscaped space in which Dulcie had built a small rockery and installed beds that were just starting to show the first shoots of flowers.

Only half an hour earlier I had been inspecting a badger sett, alone, overheated from the walk, looking for a fresh spring from which to fill my flask, yet here I was sitting at a table – something I had not done for weeks – having tea in the garden of a woman unlike any I knew back at home.

In the distance I could just make out the line of the North Sea, a faraway performance seen through binoculars in the Elysian afternoon haze.

'No plan is a good plan,' she said after some time had passed. 'You never know what's around the corner. A morning's sunny spell can harbour an afternoon's storm clouds. Life is long when you're young and short when you're old, but tenuous at any time.'

We fell silent for a moment, and the dog sighed.

'Mind, they're a rum bunch down there,' she continued.

'Who's that?'

Dulcie put down her cup and nodded towards the sea. 'That lot down bay. You have to watch them. Some are descended from smugglers. They've lived too long at sea. It has sent them funny. They're as right as rain physically but their minds have turned to mush, you see. There's a few laggards about the place.'

She took a sip and sniffed the air, then continued.

'They're not all bad, it's just that the gene pool can be more like a rock pool at low tide, if you get what I mean.'

I didn't. Instead I merely stared blankly back at her. I saw a woman in odd flowing clothes that were either extremely old-fashioned and of another era entirely, or the height of modern fashion; I was unequipped to judge either way. Even the swirling colours of the scarf she wore and her billowing trousers – *trousers* – seemed to be taken from a different palette. I noticed that her hands were long and mapped with thick veins, and though her nails were painted they also showed signs of having been plunged in the soil.

'And some of the old sea dogs sup like fish. You should see them: bellies like ale barrels. It's a wonder they can see anything when the garden needs watering.'

I nodded as Dulcie watched me sideways. When I realised what it was she meant I blushed and then smiled.

'Still, no harm in them. No harm in them *at all*. No doubt some of them think I'm an ageing ungodly slattern or Satan himself, but heck, they can go whistle.'

'Do you not believe in God, then – ' Here once more my mouth faltered as I found myself unable to call her, an adult, by her first name: Dulcie.

She made a noise in response. 'Hmmph. Buck and fugger to that. We've got more than our fair share of Bible-thumpers round here as it is. The old joyless fire-and-brimstone-and-two-fucks-a-lifetime Christian lot.'

I flinched at the word that even most of the miners I knew reserved only for certain all-male company, and which even then was frowned upon. Shocked by this confident and intimidating lady, I felt myself flailing. I was out of my conversational depth. She was quite unlike my mother or most older women I knew, who certainly wouldn't swear and blaspheme in the same sentence. I was used to a subdued and unquestioning reverence towards religion, especially from the elderly.

'No,' she continued, 'I'm of the opinion that religion is nothing but end-of-the-pier hocus-pocus. You might as well spend an hour with Gypsy Rose Lee as sit through a dull Sunday-morning service.'

I was shocked to hear an opinion of which Dulcie seemed so certain that to dispute it might make me appear ignorant. A strange prickling ripple of tension crept across my scalp at the thought. Quite casually she was turning those theological teachings drummed into me during banal daily assemblies upside down and giving them a good shake.

'Are you a believer?' she asked.

'I'm Church of England.'

'And what does that mean, exactly?'

I thought about this for a moment. 'Well, it means I went to a C of E school.'

Dulcie smiled. 'And what does that mean?'

Again I thought about her question. I smiled back. 'A lot of daydreaming.'

'Daydreaming is good.'

'The teachers didn't think so.'

'I'm sure they didn't, but from the dreams of children come the great empires of the future. You strike me as someone who spent as much time looking out the window as you did at the textbook page.'

'I was probably looking at the pit, where my dad works – and his dad before him.'

'Ah, a coalman.'

'Well, the coalman delivers. My dad works the seam. He's a miner.'

'Digging out the dusky diamonds, as they say. And what about you?'

'What about me?'

'Will you follow your forefathers underground?'

'I don't know,' I said, though it was of course a question I had been forced by circumstance and expectation to contemplate for years. 'I thought I'd take a wander first. The pits aren't going anywhere. There'll always be mining. There'll always be coal.'

'That's certainly true. What else did you do at this school of yours?'

'I sat through long assemblies and lots of tuneless hymns.'

'That's it?'

'Harvest festival in September and Christmas carol services. That's about it.'

'Well, harvest worship is a pagan practice for starters and many of the Christmas traditions are pre-Christian and have been synchronised and co-opted, but that's by the by. Children aren't to know. None of this has a thing to do with faith or what some might call spirituality, which is something else entirely. Butler doesn't much care for religion either.'

'No?'

'He bit the last vicar that tried to pat him. They said he should be put down but just let the bastards try.'

The sun stalked across the sky, lighting the meadow that once must have offered a clear vista of the open fields but which now felt like a barrier, an uncultivated plot to keep the sea partially concealed as the sun scattered silver triangles across its surface.

The drying sweat on my back and the stiff reek of my clothes – for weeks I had washed only from outdoor wells and under farmyard spouts – reminded me that the swim I had been planning for some time seemed close at hand, yet the sea was tantalisingly obscured from view behind that chaotic acre of grasses and hawthorns, weeds and thicket.

The nettle tea was refreshing, though, and the biscuits that Dulcie served were the first sweet food other than foraged berries and a flapjack in Guisborough that had passed my lips in a fortnight. I felt the sugar coursing through my blood.

We sat in silence for a few moments before she checked her watch and then spoke.

'You should stay for tea. Proper tea, I mean.'

Mindful of my own body odour and a need to find somewhere to bed down for the night, I declined her invitation. 'It's very kind of you but this was more than enough. I should really push on.'

'That's your prerogative. But may I ask where it is you intend to push on *to*, exactly? Unless you think I'm prying.'

'I thought I'd perhaps go down to the bay and then follow the coast south.'

The dog appeared by Dulcie's side and she scratched behind his ears.

'*Le grand tour*,' she said. 'You know, locals tend to simply say "down bay". There are sights to be seen, for sure. Fossils and hermit crabs and creels and the sea chipping away at Britannia's boundary. But there's nothing that still won't be there later. The tide will ebb and the tide will flow, the bladderwrack will rise and reach for the saffron stain of the sun and the seagulls will swoop for some poor sod's chips. I'm doing lobster, not that I am attempting to keep you captive. Do you partake?'

I sat straight with my shirt stuck to my back and my back pressed against the chair. My hands felt self-conscious in my lap, grubby and without purpose. The nails chewed to the quick. I folded my fingers to hide the shame of them.

'I've not had lobster before, no.'

Dulcie looked mock-aghast. 'Never?'

'My mam's not big on fish.'

Sensing perhaps that my restricted diet was as much down to economics as availability, Dulcie was discreet. 'Well, God knows this war has made us all tighten our belts,' she said. 'We might have our freedom but a tin of pilchards still seems like a luxury.'

'It's those Germans,' I said quietly. 'I'd like to give them what for.'

'Would you?'

'Yes, they should all rot for what they've done. You should see some of the men in the village. And that's just the ones who made it back. I'd slit the throat of any Kraut, me. It would be my duty as an Englishman.'

40

Dulcie studied me for a moment.

'I can understand your hatred completely,' she said. 'And your spirited *Boy's Own* bravado is to be applauded. But, Robert, you should not be bitter or angry about it. War is war: it's started by the few and fought by the many, and everyone loses in the end. There's no glory in bloodshed and bullet holes. Not a bit of it. I also happen to know that Germany has been left in a terrible state too, and always remember that most of those young men – boys the same age as you are now, no doubt – did not want to be there either. It's always the honest folk that have to do the bidding of the despots. And after all there are only a few things truly worth fighting for: freedom, of course, and all that it brings with it. Poetry, perhaps, and a good glass of wine. A nice meal. Nature. Love, if you're lucky. And that's about it. Don't hate the Germans; many of them are just like you and me.'

Having read the morning newspaper reports and heard the evening wireless broadcasts, and endured the long fearful years of gas masks and air-raid drills, of rationing and dirt-dug shelters, and seen the men who made it back to the village – some limping, others trembling, all of them changed – I couldn't see how this could possibly be true. I had grown from a boy to a young man knowing few certainties in life; that the Germans were surely a monstrous breed was one of them. I failed to see how they could possibly be like us. Dulcie saw me frowning.

'You don't agree?'

'I just find that hard to believe.'

'And who can blame you: all you have known is war's long shadow, and all the trumpeting and chest-thumping that goes along with it. But I have seen other wars. Read about plenty more too. And what I've learned is that they're all much the same: people are people. I speak this from experience. Some are brave and some are foolish, and almost all are scared. War is chaos, that's all. German or British, Armenian, Dutch or Tongan – most people just want a quiet life. A nice meal, a little love. A late-night stroll. A lie-in on a Sunday. As I said before, don't despise the Germans. All that really separates us is a different approach to bread-making and *that*.'

Here she pointed out towards the sea. 'It's only water that divides us, and even that came later on. Once, you could have walked from here all the way to Bremen or Leipzig or Hanover or wherever your feet happened to take you. Doggerland, they called it. One day the salty water simply washed over the last strip of land to sluice away the soil and – *voilà* – a new island was created. Think about that for a moment: once England was Germany and vice versa.'

I slowly nodded, chewing over this new fact.

'We're all just people, Robert. We're all confused, lonely and flawed, but a fine fresh lobster lifted from the briny depths of Dogger is the definition of perfection, and seeing as this conversation has held us in the hinterland of the afternoon I am now going to insist that you stay on for an hour or so. Then, after you're fed, you can sail to the Fatherland with a dagger between your teeth if you so wish. Besides, Butler here is a German shepherd and he's the most loyal friend an old sturgeon like me could wish for. I must have a thing for Teutons.'

At this, the dog stepped forward and sniffed at my knuckles. I patted his warm noble head.

'I think he's readying himself to accept you.'

'Thank you,' I said. 'Thank you, I will stay for tea.'

'You can thank me by fetching a good clump of garlic from down the meadow. It's the perfect garniture for just about everything that passes my lips; little wonder I live alone. Now, I'll nip out and get the crustaceans.' Dulcie stood and straightened her sun hat. 'Butters will show you where to find it.' She instructed the dog – 'Butters, *garlic*' – and then laughed at her own wordplay as he cocked his large head upwards.

Dulcie walked towards the side of the cottage, then paused.

'The Germans call it *Blasentang*, you know.'

I was confused. 'Garlic?'

'No, bladderwrack. A good source of vitamins. And iodine too. I'll get those lobsters.'

———

As I followed the dog beyond the garden fence and into the overgrown field I heard a voice calling to me. I turned and saw Dulcie waving a pair of secateurs.

She shouted something that I couldn't make out.

'What?'

'Watch out for the spring,' she said. She pointed with the metal blades. 'The spring. The waterhole. Further down. Watch out for the sudden drop in the grass. Butters knows where it is.'

I followed the sight line to where she was pointing and carefully picked my way down through the meadow. It was deep with weeds. Within twenty paces in any direction I counted balsam, ragwort, nipplewort, knotweed, bindweed, chickweed, aster, nettles, brambles, burdock, cleavers, thistles of various sizes – some sprouting to shin height. I recognised other plants too: sedge, valerian, foxglove and harebells as well as the usual abundance of dandelions and all manner of wildflowers such as ox-eye daisy, flax and roseroot. It was remarkable how many different species had made their way to the wild meadow, and all vying for the same small patch of sky.

Sure enough the ground slipped away to a small submerged spring bubbling up into the long grass and gently flooding a lower patch of the land before flowing further down the field to find the shortest way to the sea. It was little more than a trickle.

The dog pushed on, impervious to the burrs that stuck to his fur, or the nettles that brushed his maw, and he flattened a path to a bosky patch where there were gathered dozens of bouquets of wild garlic, sprouting like leafy fountains from the soil.

I crouched down, tore at a leaf and folded it into my mouth. The garlic's white flowers had not yet blossomed and, unsure as to whether it was the leaves or bulbs I was collecting, I found a short stick and used it to carefully scrape away the soil so that I could lift several whole plants, their thin pale roots hanging from the base of their rounded white edible stems.

Down in this shaded corner I could see neither the sea nor the cottage, which, with the creeper crawling across its facade, already gave the impression of being pulled down into the Yorkshire sandstone. Held in the clutches of this hollow, I had in that moment the impression of the meadow being entirely sealed off from the world.

I felt an enlivening and distorting of the senses, strange but not without pleasure, as if I were experiencing the wildlife around me to a heightened and intense degree. And not only experiencing it, but becoming a part of it, immersed in such a way that I could hear the rustle of every crawling ant or the scratching of each fly's dry wing, or the chewing of a masticating wasp on a rotten piece of timber hidden from view. Breathing deeply, I smelled the sod, the garlic, herbs and airborne pollen, and the tang of the salted sea air too. A meal of the senses. The tiniest details came into sharp focus: the skeletal architecture of a small dead leaf that had lain untouched since winter, or the quiver of a solitary blade of wild grass where others beside it were still. The gentle panting of the dog too fell into the rhythm of my own heart as it beat a gentle pattern of sweet coursing blood in my eardrums. A single drop of sweat ran down my left temple. I felt alive. Gloriously, deliriously alive.

For what felt like hours, but may in fact have only been a few seconds, time appeared static, the moment frozen, until I finally stood and, with garlic in hand, and the dog pushing past me, felt delirious from sensation, and then took a narrow trail deeper downhill through the thickening grass. It led between some brambles and brought me to a rotten gate that hung from one rusted hinge. I pushed through it and found myself at the edge of a much flatter farmed field that looked right out across the descending land. Here, finally, was the sea, in its full, unobstructed aspect.

At the far end of the field a horse with thick fetlocks raised its head for a moment and then resumed tugging at the cud, the flat shape of its silhouette form framed by the vast body of shimmering water behind it. The horse appeared to be suspended there between the strips of blue and green that were the sky, the sea and the field.

The dog stood alongside, accepting of my presence, and I let time and landscape wash around me, the hum of insects and the coda of nearby birdsong the closing soundtrack to an afternoon reverie of such power and potency that my whole life was, perhaps, imperceptibly nudged in a different direction.

III

Walking back, I saw tucked away in the top corner of Dulcie Piper's meadow, adjacent to her house and secreted beneath an overhang of branches, a sunken structure which, like the cottage, gave the impression of being pulled under.

I pushed through the grass towards what was a shack, an old summer house perhaps, constructed from creosote-coated wood, now unevenly shaped from decades of sun, salt, fret and neglect, but nevertheless standing soundly on a raised base of solid stone. The steeply arched corrugated roof was stained acidic cobalt in colour from decades of rain and patched with a thick rug of moss. The sheets of lead lining were intact on its apex, and the ornately rendered white window frames, though weathered, had all their glass in place. One old clay drainpipe hung loose, broken, leading to nowhere.

I tried the door. It was held shut by the encroachment of wildlife from the meadow. I attempted to shoulder it open but the warped wood had jammed it in the frame so instead I cupped my hands around my eyes and saw inside a place of dust and darkness.

Though the bespoke joinery and ornate finishings suggested something more than a mere tool shed, it was now nothing but a neglected storage space for items never needed. There was an old bedspring frame in there, and a dresser. On the floor were some wadded rags, cardboard boxes matted damp with age, an old suitcase, a tin can containing an assortment of screws, nails and wing nuts. I saw a rattan chair with oversized holes picked through it, as if gnawed at by rodents. There was a standing lamp with neither shade nor bulb and many stubbed thumbs of melted candles were stuck to the interior windowsills, their wax drippings hanging pendulously, or hardened into phlegmy globules on the stained floorboards below them. There were curled sheets of paper, discarded in the corner. A couple of empty wine bottles. And dust. Dust everywhere.

Dulcie called me then and, true to his name, the dog reappeared a moment later by my side to guide me like a discreet but attentive valet. Mindful of disturbing an established hierarchy, I let him lead the way.

She was gesturing from the kitchen, a veil of steam billowing up from the pot that was noisily roiling away. She pushed the window open wider. 'Come in and look at these beautiful beasts,' she said.

I walked around to the side door and stepped into the kitchen. It was small, like the galley of a ship, with pots and pans and utensils hanging everywhere from hooks, and was dominated by an old scorched range that featured several circular hotplates, a main oven and two side ovens. It seemed like something from another age, a roaring fire pit emitting more heat than the warm day needed.

All around there were unlit candles placed on saucers and in old sardine tins, and from the ceiling hung a paraffin lamp on which Dulcie, a good three inches taller than me, almost certainly must have hit her head with regularity.

'Have you been down to the bay and back already?' I asked. 'Sorry, I mean *down bay*.'

'Not likely. Barton brings them up. Twice a week he leaves a couple in the water trough out on the lane. Fish too. Haddock, plaice, skate. Whatever the catch can spare. A jar of whelks. Even the odd eel sometimes. I live off the stuff. It puts pep in your step. Good for the brain too. Look – '

I bent over the boiling pot and saw two lobsters like craggy creatures lifted from prehistoric times turning a darkening umber colour in the bubbling pan.

'They're huge,' I said.

'Actually they're small. But the smaller ones have the sweeter meat. The bigger ones are older and don't always taste as pure. *Their* flesh has turned cynical.'

'Their claws are mismatched.'

'Yes, you see that one is the pincer for holding and the other is the crusher for – well, that's self-explanatory.'

'Do they nip?'

'Wouldn't you if manhandled out of your bed in the midst of a bloody good sleep?'

I smiled. 'Yes, I reckon I would. In fact, it has happened once or twice recently thanks to one or two unfriendly landowners.'

'Cretins.'

Dulcie crouched and opened the range door and threw in two logs, which she prodded into place with a poker, then closed it again.

'Who's Barton?' I asked.

'A fisherman. Shadrach Barton III, to give him his full name. He lives up the hill. A nice chap. He gives the impression of being taciturn but I think he's just more at ease on the water than he is on the land. He has a permanent squint from perennially scouring the water for fishing grounds. A good singing voice too, by all accounts. Shanties mainly, but Christ, the songs go on and on. Now: garlic.'

Dulcie put out her hand and I passed the garlic to her. She quickly trimmed away the leaves and sliced the roots down to the bare bulbs. These she skinned and diced, and then she placed a small pan on the hob.

'Does he bring you the logs too?'

'Heavens, no.' She nodded out across the back garden to where I noticed for the first time a sawhorse and chopping block. 'It keeps me trimble,' she said. 'Trim and nimble. They always say logs warm you up three times: chopping them, carrying them and burning them.'

From her pantry in the corner she brought out an enormous butter dish from which she cut a knob the size of a small bar of soap and dropped it into the pan. That piece alone constituted more than the two ounces per week that I knew the rationing book allowed.

'We'll have white. Can you get me a bottle?' Dulcie nodded towards the pantry.

It was cool in there, and I saw stacked in a rack at least two, perhaps three, dozen bottles of wine, both red and white. There were other bottles too, containing spirits I had never tasted. Whisky, cognac, gin, plus cherry brandy and ones labelled with words I had never seen: GRAPPA, SCHNAPPS and METAXA.

From floor to ceiling the shelves were packed with tins of meat and fish and beans and soup, and different bags of flour – buckwheat and rye – plus sugar and rice, and packets of biscuits and bars of chocolate. There were two large dried sausages and jars featuring various seasonings, chutneys, pickles and preserves. Some of the labels appeared to be in German. There were boxes too, containing exotic-looking delicacies such as figs and dates and Turkish delight, and bottles of cooking oil and fruit cordial. As well as the large bowl of butter, there was also a tray of twenty or more eggs and two small wheels of cheese wrapped in green leaves. On the floor in a wooden crate there were fruits and vegetables. I saw apples, carrots, potatoes, kale, celery, spring onions.

An imposter in a stranger's house, and surrounded by all this produce, I felt overwhelmed, disjointed somehow, as if I had once again stepped into a picture or a painting.

'Most of the wine is pre-war,' Dulcie said, quite oblivious to these odd and conflicting sensations I was experiencing. 'I stocked up. Forward-thinking. I'm down to the vinegary dregs now and the entire rack is in need of purgation. I even have a bottle of Lindisfarne Mead that is probably as old as Cuthbert's corpse. Most of the wine is passable, though too much will tend to sour the stomach.'

I lingered in the pantry a moment longer. I had never seen such variety of food and drink in one place. Back at home there was the butcher, the greengrocer and so on but even the general store had the same unchanging supply of ration food: tinned English hams, baked beans, loose tea, sweaty government cheese, patties of lard that looked like engine grease and jars of jam that was rumoured to be made from discarded root vegetables.

Dulcie saw me marvelling at all that food. 'I have friends in places both high and low, and several in foreign climes,' she said by way of an explanation. 'Until they let us buy what we want again, I shall continue to call upon their generosity.'

Having never tasted wine, I had no idea which to select so picked a bottle of white at random.

'Do you think it'll go on much longer?'

She shrugged. 'The war may be won, but the battle against bland food continues apace. And I, for one, shall not be defeated.'

I passed the bottle to Dulcie but she only glanced at the label as she stirred the liquefying butter and scraped the garlic in.

'Good choice. Will you open it? The corkscrew's in the drawer.'

I found the implement and fumbled with it. Wedging it between my knees, I managed to uncork my first bottle of wine without breaking the cork or spilling it down myself. Dulcie took it from me, splashed a dash into the butter and then took a larger swig directly from the bottle.

She smacked her lips.

'You know, Robert, I've got so used to dining with just Butler watching on that I've forgotten my manners. Forgive me. Glasses – two, please.'

She poured the wine and then we clinked drinks. I took a large mouthful and swallowed it down quickly. There was a sharpness followed by a warm sensation that spread through my gullet and chest and deep down into my stomach. It was the first liquid I had tasted that appeared *dry*, though the feeling was not completely disagreeable. I took another swig and felt the wine in my veins as a pleasant ache. The stove was kicking out a lot of heat.

Dulcie lifted the large pot and poured away the water. 'These lobs are done,' she said. With tongs she lifted them onto plates and passed them to me. 'We'll eat al fresco.'

'Great,' I said, not moving. 'Lovely.'

'Outside?'

'Oh, right.'

Dulcie followed me with a small bowl of the garlic butter and another containing the chopped leaves. There was a board with half a loaf on it already there, two flies atop it.

As I sat stiff and straight at the table she passed me a nutcracker. 'I'll show you how,' she said, pushing up her sleeves. 'Some people eat the legs, but claw, knuckle and tail is where you'll find the best meat. Now, watch.'

Dulcie took a claw and twisted it away from the body of the lobster, which was now a deep burnt orange in colour, steam plumes rising from the fissures where its limbs joined its body. It looked almost like a toy, a macabre stage prop.

Here she paused and looked me up and down. She shook her head. 'You're going to have to loosen up, you know. Look at you: you're stiff as a lighthouse keeper's prick. At ease, soldier.'

She then gently but deftly pulled back the smaller jaw of the pincer until it broke away, revealing a cuticle-shaped crescent of pure white flesh. She dipped this twice in the garlic butter and then tipped it to her mouth, pulling the meat from the shell. Then she folded a piece of bread into her mouth after it, chased it with a gulp of wine, and took the nutcracker back from me and used it to crack the main claw, carefully picking off two or three tiny flecks of the broken shell. A hunk of flesh fell onto the plate. She skewered some garlic leaves then split the claw meat with the edge of her fork and twice dipped the whole lot into the butter again, and then ate it, chewing noisily and making a sound of satisfaction: *mmm-hmmn.*

'Food of the gods,' she said through a mouthful, as a stray fleck of green garlic leaf worked its way out of her mouth, hung there for a moment and then fell to the table.

Dulcie smacked her lips, smiled and picked up more bread.

'Dig in, Robert, before it makes a break for it.'

I followed her lead and managed to extract the warm flesh from the lobster that just that morning, as I was waking and stretching in the shadow of hedgerow, damp and stiff and cursing the dawn chorus, had been ambling along the seabed somewhere out there, where the rising sun refracted in the upper reaches and all life danced in its warming rays.

I dipped it into melted butter that was the colour of egg yolk and just as creamy, and then held the piece of lobster there in my mouth. I didn't even have to chew: it collapsed into a soft paste, with only the faintest hint of the sea behind it. Never had I tasted anything fresher; the kippers that my mam reluctantly fried for my dad on a Friday were old leathery things in comparison, like the inner sole of a pitman's boot, the scent of the smokehouse lingering all weekend long.

Next we ate the meat from the knuckles on hunks of bread topped with garlic leaves and double-dipped again.

'The wine,' she said. 'You haven't touched your wine.'

I took another sip and let it wash around my mouth. It was still too tart for my liking, but the salted aftertaste of the butter seemed to take the sickle-sharp edge off it.

'We save the best bit for last.'

Dulcie took the lobster from her plate in both hands and in one move she bent the tail up from the body and separated it. A large thick thumb of meat extended, shucked from the curved shell like a creature peeking from a hole.

'Look,' she said. 'See that greenish paste inside? That's the liver. Good in soups or sauces. We can eat that too. Those that have a red coral-like matter inside are female; that's the roe. Also edible. But this is a male. We just need to remove this thing.'

Here she pulled out a long stringy vein, which she cast aside into the garden.

'For the birds or beasts. Or Butler.'

I followed suit and discovered the meat from the tail to be even sweeter. We ate more bread and garlic butter and finished off a rough salad. Dulcie poured more wine and we sat in silence.

'So,' said Dulcie, 'you're here to see the sea.'

'Yes. Back at home it turns grey with dust and people pick the coal that washes in on the tide straight from the beach, great sacks of it that they stack on their carts, but down here it is different and the sand looks so much cleaner too. We live too far inland to visit much, though close enough to hear the seagulls. It feels nice to be nearer the water for a while.'

The meadow and the wine had loosened my tongue somewhat and I found myself talking more than I was accustomed to in the company of strangers, or anyone.

'That is very true,' said Dulcie. 'Though if you keep going you'll hit Hull and the Humber and, beyond that, Grimsby. They might change your mind.'

'I thought I would see Scarborough first. Maybe get some work there.'

'Doing what?'

'Doing anything. Perhaps some busking.'

'Music, you mean? Do you play?'

I reached into my pocket and pulled out the Jew's harp. I put it to my lips and started plucking a tuneless melody.

Dulcie beamed, and then laughed. 'I know this one: *Oh, I do like to be beside the seaside.*'

I began to quicken my tweaking of the instrument and my intake of breath, so that it strayed from the original familiar melody and began to make a guttural drone which I speeded up, faster and faster, throwing in staccato rhythmic noises. It sounded like an irritant, a trapped wasp, but over the past few weeks I had practised enough to pluck out something that was occasionally recognisable.

'Wonderful,' she said. 'Well done you, and a very wise move to play the old *tiddley-om-pom-pom* favourites.

I'd chuck a coin in your cap if I were passing; I'm sure others will do the same, especially if you can master "We'll Meet Again" or that God-awful "White Cliffs of Dover" song. Strike for sentiment, I'd say. You can't fail. Here, do you know how Scarborough got its name?'

'No. I don't think so.'

'Not many people do,' said Dulcie. 'But then some people never bother to read a book in their entire lives – I don't mean you, you're out doing something even better: you're living life. But there are some out there for whom even the newspaper is only good for soaking up chip fat and cat scat. Anyway, it got its name from two Vikings, Thorgils and Kormak Ögmundarson. Or one of them, anyway.'

'I don't quite understand how Scarborough was named after the Vikings.'

'I was getting to that.'

'Sorry.'

Dulcie smiled over her glass. 'Only be sorry for the things you regret. Well, anyway. They were brothers, Thorgils and Kormak. Real rotten apples but, you know, in Viking society that could sometimes be deemed an asset, for back then moral codes were quite different to ours today.'

Dulcie drained her glass and then poured more wine for herself and took a large noisy gulp.

'In 966 AD, having determined to write the Sagas with fists and hatchets alone, these two brothers stocked up their longboats and with a small army of strong men in tow left their homeland behind in search of adventure and bounty – a bit like you and your epic voyage, in fact.'

'I'm not sure if it's an epic voyage. More of a holiday, really.'

'Travel is a search for the self, trust me. And sometimes just to search is enough.'

'Do you think so?'

'Of course. Wander around long enough with your eyes open and soon enough you'll find things. Great journeys are never about the destination.'

'Yes,' I said. 'I mean, this morning I didn't imagine I'd taste lobster, lemon or wine by evening.'

'Exactly. *Exactly.* That's precisely what I'm talking about: open eyes. Experience. But I'm digressing. These brothers. Well, they sailed south through choppy ice-cold seas to undertake a series of show-no-mercy raids on the coast of Britain.'

'Where did they sail from?' I wondered.

'I'm not sure. If I had to hazard a guess I would say Iceland. *Ögmundarson* suggests the Icelandic tradition of men adding the "-son" suffix to their father's first name. So, for example, Thorgils and Kormak would be recognised as the sons of Ögmundar. Thorgils and Kormak Ögmundarson. And you would be – what's your father called?'

'Ronald.'

'Perfect: then you would be Robert Ronaldson, a Viking-sounding name if ever there was one. So Iceland was where these two brothers sailed from and upon arrival on these foreign shores they upturned their longboats and lived under them for a while, and then, in time, they established a stronghold in a dramatic sweep of conjoined bays backed by the verdant slopes right here on this very coast. They named this settlement *Skarthaborg*, from Thorgils' nickname, *Skarthi*, meaning "Harelip".'

'Harelip?'

'Oh, yes. You see, Thorgils had been born with this facial disfigurement and actually it had only served to make him a better Viking. All the childhood teasing had made him bitter, angry and violent – perfect warrior material. "Just stoke him up and watch him blaze," the other Vikings used to say, and then they would laugh from deep within their whale skins.'

'The poor lad,' I said.

'Well, maybe. Sometimes you just had to *look* at Thorgils the wrong way and he'd skin you with his billhook. So let's hold back on our sympathy, for the suffering Thorgils inflicted on others far outweighed the cruel ribbing he experienced from his hirsute contemporaries. Violence, arson, theft, rape, murder – these were not gentlemen, and everything they gained was through brute force alone. They didn't need an invitation to enter anyone's home or marital bed, that's for sure.'

'We did a lesson on the Vikings.'

'Then you probably know this already,' said Dulcie. 'It seems at "Harelip" they enjoyed good fishing and good times with those local women who had not managed to flee the area. Like I said, Thorgils and Kormak

Ögmundarson were bad boys but successful Vikings. And sure enough they were soon breeding, and this small stronghold of theirs grew into a community and that community became first a village and then a town that spread right across the two bays. Of course, this took many centuries of conflict and dispute and setbacks, and the Ögmundarson brothers were, after all, mortals, who didn't stick around long enough to see such an expansion, though they live on in the genes of many in Britain today. Many, many centuries passed to bring us to the spa seaside resort that it is today, Skarthaborg, otherwise known as Scarborough, around one thousand years after the Ögmundarsons first salted a cod there and Thorgils Ögmundarson brained Bjarni Sigmundsson with a rusty oarlock for calling him *Skarthi* one time too many.'

'Who is Bjarni Sigmundsson?'

'That doesn't matter.'

Night settled upon the meadow like a trawler's net sinking slowly to the deeper waters, the sun fading as the gloom enfolded everything within it.

The evening had drained into night as we had drained the bottle of wine, and it was too late to continue down bay, where there would be nowhere but doorways and ginnels in which to sleep, or the beach, where the incoming tide could take a sleeping man away.

So at the top end of the meadow I pegged my tarp into a triangular shape and crawled in with my sleeping bag and a small flask of tea dashed with a tot of whisky that Dulcie had insisted I bring with me. She had also offered Butler's service as a nightwatchman but I had declined. I did not fear the dark. In fact, I relished it.

It was a clear, crisp night and it had cooled considerably as I lay watching the sky run the gamut of blues, my head swimming from the wine and my stomach bloated and creaking from the rich buttery food after several weeks of dining on the scavenged basics.

An elongated prism of light stretched from an upper window of Dulcie's cottage across the garden and beyond the border fence into the meadow, but soon that went out and all was perfect darkness. But darkness is never a solid mass and in time the shapes of the swaying branches of distant trees distinguished themselves, and the night became a thing of layers, a lamination of changing hues in which perspective becomes distorted and suddenly judgement itself is placed under question. Foreground and background appeared to swap places, and the night offered a series of mesmerists' illusions in this dark velvet theatre ruled by creatures of blood and bone.

I tuned into the changing soundtrack as the daytime residents were replaced by those nocturnal species who turned the meadow into an arena of feeding, flying, calling and crawling. The late shift had begun, and the creatures of the night slowly tuned up like the school orchestra reconvening after a long break. Fluttering moths tapped out paradiddle rhythms with their dry wings at the dull lamp that hung at the end of Dulcie's lane, and the dipping shadow-shapes of bats clicked as they swooped down to snatch them up by the dozen, flitting in irregular, jerking circles, frenziedly feeding while mapping the night.

Field mice carved the tiniest curving tunnelled runs through the grass, and a barn owl watched on silently from its treetop promontory. I followed the sound of its call with my eyes and stared into the darkening blue for several minutes before I saw its shape on the branch and then, fleetingly, its wide unblinking eyes like two moons crossed by a passing streak of threadbare cloud.

And in that moment I felt something of a kinship with those lone sailors and fishermen out on the sea's skyline who had only their twinkling lamplights to register their existence, the coast of their country and the warm beds of their wives as distant as other planets – visible but unreachable, held between thumb and forefinger as they bobbed on the soft swell, anchored only by the deep ache of longing.

From further afield I heard another owl hoot, and then across the basin of land that curved its way down to the sea a lone dog barked incessantly. The whisky-tea went untouched. The night alone had me drunk enough. In time it took me entirely.

IV

I awoke to a different symphony.

The night shift had been replaced by a new menagerie of sun-worshipping species intent on serenading me from the first glimpsed finger of light that scratched at the roaring dawn sky.

From branches and nests and hedgerows and the meadow their calling came.

I lay for a few moments and conducted a sleepy inventory of sound. There was the polyphonic throaty dual-note mantra of two resting wood pigeons, one near and one distant, twin sounds of contentment. Above that, the pedantic argument of a shrieking flock of seagulls coasting on an inland updraught, and from all around came the buzz and hum of insects hatching and insects breeding, insects taking flight and insects feeding. Ticks and bees and moths and flies. Grasshoppers and ants and beetles of many varieties; newly hatched creatures born in the dawn dew and dried by the morning's rays to rise and conquer the unfolding day. There was more dry scratching and the melodious fluttering of freshly unfurled butterfly wings thinner than any paper, more beautiful than a stained-glass window.

Across the valley I could hear distant sheep being freed from their corral, each ewe and her young twig-legged lamb in constant contact via bleated conversations, some more urgent than others. And still a solitary dog barked so insistently, and for so long, that I wondered if it were the same one I had fallen asleep to, and whether perhaps it had forgotten the reason it was even barking in the first place.

Somewhere not far away, just beyond the limits of the meadow, where pastures spread to form a mosaic of land both tilled and untouched, I heard the strangulated cough of a young roe deer, its body cautiously curled and pressed deep into vegetation, perhaps, tromped down into fresh wild grass, close enough by to be heard, yet never daring to slumber in the same place for two nights running. There was just the single gruff engine-like honk of waking contentment, then it was silenced.

Nature's alarm clock told me it was nearly time to rise. With all the noise I had little choice but I lay still for a moment longer, feeling the sun begin to warm my primitive tarpaulin tent as its rays stretched across the hillside.

I must have fallen back to sleep for when I awoke Butler the dog was standing silently at the entrance to my improvised bivouac. His head was cocked an inch or two to one side and his eyebrows arched to enhance an already expressive look. Having never owned one, I had never much noticed the behaviour of dogs before – round our streets they roamed freely, scavenging from bins, and doing their best to avoid getting flattened by the coal trucks that rumbled through the village – but I was already beginning to recognise the signs with which Dulcie's dog communicated.

'Hello, Butler,' I said. 'Good morning, dog.'

At this his ears tilted forward and he lowered his haunches, firmly planting his front paws. With the morning sun behind him, the lighter sections of his thick pelt became a rusted colour; his russet fur was dotted thereabouts with grass seeds that had lodged themselves to hitch a ride during his morning meadow-wandering, and also a small snatch of cleavers, their tiny hooked hairs giving the impression of stickiness when I leaned over to pluck them away. The dog let me groom him briefly. I tentatively scratched behind his ears and he responded by nudging my hand and half-turning away, and then repeating the action.

I understood: I was being summoned.

Though the morning air had a cool edge to it, the sun poured molten glass on the still indifferent sea and the outside table was already laid with the remains of yesterday's loaf plus pots of jam, honey and butter, and more nettle tea turning pink in the pot. There were also apples and a small jug of cream. Dulcie was sitting at the table wearing a comically wide-brimmed sun hat, with a hardback book further obscuring her face. The dog led me to the table and then lay down beneath it. It was perhaps later than I realised.

'Good morning,' I said.

Dulcie lowered the book and then shaded her eyes with one hand. 'And how did you sleep?'

'Well,' I said. 'Very heavily.'

'I thought I'd send Butler along before the cream curdled.'

'What time is it?'

'I have no idea,' she said. 'I'm afraid I don't keep a clock. The wireless or my stomach tell me what I need to know. Tea?'

'Yes, please.'

'I'm not a morning person so I will ask you just one more question and you can keep your response quite brief: would you like some eggs?'

'Oh, no. This is quite sufficient.'

'Then help yourself.'

Dulcie poured my tea and I joined her at the table, where we drank and ate in silence, occasionally swatting away the wasps that had begun to pay visits to the jam pot.

'This is very kind of you – '

Dulcie batted the compliment away as swiftly as she did the wasps.

Minutes passed and the sun rose further to slowly push back the shrinking shadows from the southern edge of the meadow.

When the bread had been eaten, and we had each had an apple, and the teapot had been drained so that all that was left was a wadded clot of nettle leaves sitting in some dirty green residue, Dulcie leaned back in her chair and closed her eyes.

'Thank you for the lack of conversation. Silence is indeed golden.'

'You're welcome,' I said.

'You don't say much, and I like that. There is poetry in silence but most don't stop to hear it. They just talk, talk, talk, but say nothing because they are afraid of hearing their own heartbeat. Afraid of their own mortality.'

Several more minutes passed before Dulcie opened her eyes.

'You know, I don't think I've slept under canvas for years. Decades, perhaps.'

'Perhaps you should try it.'

'Not likely. Does that thing keep you dry?'

'More or less. So long as I set it up right, yes.'

'But what about your ablutions?'

Once again uncertain as to the meaning of a word I had never previously heard, I hesitated, but Dulcie happily filled in the blank for me.

'Your ones and especially your twos. Your toilet business.'

'Oh.' I hesitated. 'Well, I have a trowel.'

Dulcie raised a hand. 'Say no more; we managed quite well for thousands of years without the assistance of Mr Thomas Crapper & Co. And you're warm enough in there, are you?'

'Often I light a little fire, though that's as much for the company as the heat.'

'Makes sense. Man has found comfort at the fireside since time immemorial. I believe there is evidence that humans first used fire to cook food nearly two million years ago. Astonishing.'

I took a final bite from my apple core.

'Sleeping in the meadow last night was like being in another world,' I said. 'The noises sent me to sleep and then others woke me up.'

'Yes, I do rather like the wildness of the place,' said Dulcie, shading her brow again. 'But it is getting out of hand. I mean, look – ' She pointed to the low garden fence, against which an assortment of weeds were staging an assault from the outside in. 'One day it'll eat up the garden and house and I'll be left living like you in your funny little tent, a slave to knotweed and buttercups. I'll have to send the hound out for supplies.'

A moment passed and then I spoke again.

'I had a look at that shed yesterday.'

'Shed?'

'Yes, the one over in the meadow there.'

Dulcie stood and busied herself with clearing the plates. She tipped the crusts and crumbs under the table for Butler, and then followed them with a dollop of jam, which he lapped up.

'It's in a bit of a state,' I said.

Dulcie stacked the cups and teapot onto a tray.

'It looks like the meadow is trying to steal it away too,' I added. 'But structurally it still seems sound.'

'Well, I've no use for it now.'

Dulcie frowned deep in the dark crescent cast by the brim of her sun hat.

'I thought it looked a bit nicer than your usual shed or summer house,' I said.

She said nothing and instead took the plates into the kitchen before I remembered my manners and jumped up, helping her with the remainder of the jars and the cream jug. She stacked the plates into the big stone sink, alongside those from last night.

'Perhaps I could wash up before I go,' I said. 'It's the least I can do.'

'Best to let them soak.'

'I'd like to.'

'No need. Let the warm water do the work. There's far more important things in life; once a day at the very most is more than enough. Never do more than you need to, I say. Everything in moderation except moderation and all that. Oscar Wilde.'

'You've been very kind in feeding me and letting me stay.'

Again she dismissively waved a hand vaguely in my direction. 'You slept in the meadow; it's hardly the Ritz.'

'There must be something I can do about the place before I go,' I said. 'Maybe I could fetch you your messages from down bay?'

'Oh, I have plenty to eat here, don't you worry about that.'

'The meadow, then. How about I tackle some of those weeds?'

'But don't you have somewhere to *be*, Robert? I thought you were desperate to see the sea.'

'Well, I can see the sea from here if I strain my neck. Like you said yesterday, it isn't going anywhere. It'll only take me a couple of hours to hack those weeds back a yard or two. It'll give the garden a bit of breathing space, then I'll be on my way. I've not eaten so well in weeks – or ever, come to think of it – and every other meal has been payment for work.'

'A good meal isn't payment: it's a God-given right for all men and women. But if it makes you feel worthy you can spend an hour with the sickle, for all the use it'll do. I know if I was wanting to see the world – a lot of which I have, as it happens – I would be in a hurry to get out there, rather than stick around with some dusty duffer and her dog. But by all means hack away. I'll have to pay you, I suppose.'

I smiled. 'You have already paid me with the meals.'

'And you're not listening.'

'But I thought the gardening could pay for the lobster.'

'Don't undersell yourself, Robert: your conversation and company paid for the lobster. But fine. There are tools in the lean-to round the side of the house. You'll find what you need.'

The sickle was as blunt as a fish knife but in the lean-to I also found a mouldy old sharpening stone, which I cleaned and then used to strike a gleaming smooth edge back to the chipped half-circle of steel blade.

Two summers previously I had been paid a pittance to trim the grass on the village cricket pitch and long dull days on my dad's allotment had taught me the basics of tending to a plot, so I soon set to work paring back the grass and weeds around the garden's perimeter. Grasping clumps in one hand and hacking with the other didn't do much so I took to swinging the blade as hard as I could. I worked my way along the line of the fence, noting that the woodwork was beginning to rot and it was in need of a lick of paint. Again, the salt air and the damp grass had made it blister and peel away, and white flakes fell every time I inadvertently knocked against it. It was losing the battle against the meadow. The fence was merely ornamental now. Symbolic.

Within minutes I was sweating. Stooping low and then lifting the tool above my head was putting a strain on my lower back so I returned to the lean-to and rooted around. In an old shoebox whose corner had been nibbled away I found a mouse's nest built from grass and twigs. I carefully replaced it. Right at the back of the lean-to, behind some bottles of paraffin, broken picture frames and a watering can, there was a pair of long-handled shears so old that the pivoted fulcrum had rusted into place. I looked for oil but couldn't find any, despite there being an abundance of oily cloths and a set of overalls splattered with pus coloured grease and vibrant flecks of paint. I walked round to the side door and tentatively knocked, and when there was no answer I tried a second time, louder, and then pushed the door ajar and called for Dulcie.

Her voice came down from upstairs. 'Yes, what is it?'

'Sorry – ' I said, suddenly feeling like an intruder.

'What?'

'I said sorry – '

Her head peered around the top of the stairway. 'What on earth for?'

'I just wondered if you have any oil. I need some for the tools.'

'Only cooking oil. That should do it. There's plenty in the pantry. Help yourself.'

She disappeared again.

On my way out I saw through into the small sitting room that was dominated by a huge country dresser packed with a full dinner service on display. There was a fireplace and a chair too, and stacked everywhere there were piles of books and papers and two or three empty wine bottles. Above the fire on the mantelpiece there was a photograph of a young woman – Dulcie, perhaps? Another showed two women, but they were too far away for their features to be distinguishable and I didn't want to pry. A clock ticked loudly.

I oiled the bolt on the shears and then sharpened the blades with the stone and set to work again, snipping away at the grass, weeds and nettles. For the denser patches I used the sickle again, imagining myself as an executioner of sorts, until I had cleared a run a foot wide around the fence, which I then set to widening further still. Now and then I paused to rake the cuttings, wipe my brow and catch my breath. Sometimes I stopped and moved snails, slugs or worms away from the path of the blade.

An upstairs window opened and Dulcie called to me: 'Remember: don't chuck the nettles.'

I smiled and gave her the thumbs up. I took my shirt off and hung it from the fence and then carried on with my labours.

The morning sun rolled slowly across the sky as delicate music floated out over the meadow. I stood and stretched and listened as a playful piano melody loudly introduced a plummy-voiced man singing about Germans. It drifted out from the open windows of Dulcie's cottage. She appeared in the garden and waved.

'This one's for you.'

'What?' I said, not hearing her over the music.

She held a hand to her mouth and raised her voice. 'I thought you might like to whistle while you work. It's satire.'

I walked a little closer to the house and lifted one leg and then the other over the fence.

'Noël Coward,' said Dulcie. 'This one's a small satire about showing compassion to our supposed sworn enemies. I thought it apropos to our conversation last night. Do you know it?'

'No, I don't think so.'

'That's because the BBC banned it from the airwaves. Perhaps they couldn't decide whether it was too cruel or just not cruel enough. Either way, they failed to see the funny side. He's a friend of mine.'

I put down my shears and wiped my brow again with my forearm.

'He sends me all his latest recordings,' she continued. 'Whether I want them or not. They say he was in the Black Book, you know. That was the list that the little Führer and his SS cronies drew up of all the people they intended to round up and dispense of as soon as they had invaded Britain. It was a sort of *Who's Who* of interesting upstarts. I suspect it read a little like my old address book. Let me play it again for you.'

I listened to the song for a few moments. The voice was posh and slightly effeminate, again belonging to someone from an England that was unfamiliar to me. I tried to imagine its owner hewing a seam or working a wagon or telling blue jokes at the club of a Saturday evening. I couldn't picture it.

'Why was he in particular on Hitler's list?'

She shrugged. 'Who wouldn't want to be on a list of dissidents, decadents and intolerably dangerous old fruits?'

'How many people were on it?'

'Oh, hundreds, I imagine. Possibly thousands. Anyone who was anyone. All the bores, of course, would be left off, and those who had crossed over.'

'We'd be ruled by Nazis now if they had got their way,' I said.

Dulcie shook her head, tutting. 'Worse, Robert. Much worse. We would be ruled by those remaining English stiffs employed by the Nazis to do their bidding. Chinless wonders and lickspittles. There would be no room for the poets or the peacocks, the artists or the queens. Instead we'd be entirely driven by the very wettest of civil servants – even more so than we already are. A legion of pudgy middle managers would be the dreary midwives of England's downfall. Human turds, the lot of them. Stiff, dry, human turds.'

Dulcie looked adrift for a moment. She shook her head again, then continued.

'So as you can probably imagine, an appearance on the list was the highlight of Mr Coward's career to date – to be on the cultural radar, so to speak. He'd be the first to admit that he did quite well out of the war.'

'He didn't serve?'

'Serve? Noël Coward couldn't serve an omelette. No. He spent half of it at the Savoy after they bombed his home to bits, the other half entertaining the troops – or them entertaining him. And why not, I say. Play to your strengths. Here, let me spin it one more time.'

Dulcie retreated to the house and then played the song again, only louder this time. The same plucked piano chords rang out as Noël Coward began to sing again with clear, clipped diction that enunciated every single word of a song called 'Don't Let's Be Beastly to the Germans.'

She leaned out of the window.

'Well?' she said. 'Is this the type of music you like?'

I listened to the song a little longer and heard a line about the Germans' Beethoven and Bach being worse than their bite.

'It's clever, I suppose,' I said, hesitating. 'Funny.'

'It's pith,' said Dulcie. 'Pith, piss and piffle. But anything that is banned should always be worthy of further investigation. He spends a lot of time abroad now, Noël. Jamaica, mainly. He sends long letters moaning about the heat and the quality of the gin, as if he expected it any other way.'

She withdrew into the cool interior of the house and a moment later was in the garden again.

'Are you familiar with the other popular song "Hitler Has Only Got One Whatsit"?'

I smiled as I shook my head.

'Oh, yes, you are,' said Dulcie. 'You know. One ball.'

I laughed at this. 'Yes, we used to sing it in the play-ground,' I admitted. 'Sometimes some of us sang it in assembly too but the headmaster could never work out who it was, and if he had I doubt he would have punished us for it.'

'Well, I happen to have it on good authority that there is a certain truth to it.'

'How do you mean?'

'Cryptorchidism is what I mean. An undescended testicle. As a child it seems the Führer's nut bag decided to protest the pull of gravity by staying precisely put.'

She paused and scratched her chin.

'On the right side, I believe.'

'But how could you possibly know that?'

'I was told by a very credible, highly trusted source.'

'I can't believe it.'

'Well, it's true. Also his hampton was perfectly normal despite the person it had the great misfortune to find itself attached to. And that's all I can say on the matter.' She leaned forward and tapped her nose. 'The walls have ears. Now, are you hungry yet? You must be hungry by now.'

Only then did I realise how famished I was. 'I could eat,' I said. 'Yes.'

'You should eat.'

'What time is it?'

'There you are with time again. Is your belly growling?'

'It is a bit.'

'Then the clock of your guts tells us that it's lunchtime.'

Once again we ate in the garden.

Dulcie brought out a board bearing two wedges of cheese, some fresh floury rolls still steaming from the oven, a ball of butter, boiled eggs, more apples, a half-cucumber, a stone jar of pickled onions and another of whelks. There was a pot of nettle tea, and cups with a wedge of lemon in each. I was grateful for the light breeze to cool the sweat on my brow.

I tore open a roll and filled it with egg and apple and whelks.

'An imaginative combination,' said Dulcie. 'How are you getting on with the jungle?'

I chewed a few times and swallowed before answering. 'There's so much of it. I feel like I've barely made a dent.'

'I did warn you.'

'It's going to take a little longer than I expected.'

'Leave it,' she said. 'Let the next winter clear it. Let the frost do its worst. Life is limited, why fill it with toil?'

'I quite enjoy it, actually. I thought I'd just finish the fence line and then quickly trim back some of the scrub down at the bottom so that you can see the sea again.'

Dulcie reached for an apple and cut a slice from it.

'Why would I want to do that?'

She put the apple in her mouth.

'I don't know, really. Because – '

'Because, as Mallory remarked when pressed upon his reason for scaling Mount Everest, *it's there*. But there's no need. I know it's there. The tide takes it out a hundred feet and then drags it a hundred feet back in. Day after day. I don't need to see it to believe it.'

'But don't you want to enjoy the full view?'

She frowned. 'Not especially. I have no great love for the sea these days.'

'Yet you live so close to it.'

'Let's just say we had a falling-out and leave it at that.'

Dulcie chewed another slice of crisp apple.

'But how can you fall out with the sea?'

'Because you just can,' she said, a little more sternly than I expected.

We fell silent.

'I noticed your kitchen tap is dripping,' I said. 'The washer has probably gone.'

'Yes,' Dulcie said vaguely, distracted. 'I expect it has.'

'I could replace it for you.'

She ignored my deliberate attempt to steer the course of the conversation. She had other ideas.

'Look, I refuse to be at the mercy of the sea's changing whims, Robert. That's all. I just won't do it. The sea is petulant and tempestuous and I have no patience for its daily dramas. Also, sometimes – a lot of the time, in fact – it is just plain bland. The same drab story told over and over again. It tastes of the earth's detritus. It doesn't interest me.'

'It's fine. I won't trim the scrub if you don't want me to, Dulcie.'

A moment passed. She sighed.

'I know you're just trying to help. Forgive me. Here you are, practically held captive when you want to be out there, feeling the pull of the lunar tide. It's just that apart from giving up its bountiful lobsters, crabs and tunny, the sea has done me few favours over time. You shouldn't let my cynicism sour your experience, though.'

I decided not to press the issue so we sat sipping our cooling tea and digesting our meal in silence.

'I was thinking of taking a quick walk before I finish up,' I said. 'Do you think Butler would like to come?'

'I think he'd bite your arm off for a walk. He's got rather used to skulking about the place these days or watching the lane like a sentinel guard and I'm afraid his territory has become rather limited. But why don't we ask him all the same? Everyone is equal around here.' Dulcie shifted in her seat. '*Butters*. Where is that blasted – oh, there you are. Would you like to go for a walk?'

At this the dog's ears pricked up and tilted. He gave a small whine of anticipation and his tongue lolled.

'I'd say that's a yes, wouldn't you?'

She tossed him a piece of buttered bread, and then a slice of apple, and a whelk dripping vinegar, all of which he greedily gulped in turn.

'Shall I fetch his lead?' I asked.

'Oh, he doesn't need a lead, does old Butters. He's as faithful and reliable as a chaiwala, aren't you, boy? He's not one to wander off. He knows he's living the *dolce vita* right here.'

———

Any lingering wisps of morning cloud had cleared as I climbed the back fence behind Dulcie Piper's cottage and dropped into a series of conjoined fields sloping up towards the skyline. Butler vaulted the fence like a thoroughbred racehorse and darted ahead, his long wide tongue pink and coarse as it flapped about his face.

I rose out of the cleft in which the cottage and the meadow sat, and the land once again opened out. Behind me was a billowing blanket of life rippling down to the clustered fishermen's houses of the bay, and then beyond that nothing but miles of sea, which from this elevation appeared perfectly calm beneath the shallow breath of a sighing afternoon's sky.

Observed from above, the cottage sat in a hollow that had most likely been carved by many millennia of running water, the last dribbled remains of the molten ice mountains that once covered the face of Britain, and the sea around it too. As I had already seen, these slopes were shot through with wooded dells and shallow streams in which sticklebacks hovered and darted, and where the water crossed a track or road, a ford had been laid for first horses and their carts, and then automobiles.

There had been no attempt to divert the natural run of the water, or send it underground, unseen, as might happen in a town or city, but instead life had adapted to exist alongside these arterial waterways through which the hundreds of square miles of open marshy moorlands above drained to meet the salt water of the sea in a cocktail of stewed-looking peat water and heavy brine.

Here I could look upon Dulcie's cottage, shrunk down to the size of a toytown abode, with its red-tiled roof and parasitic plants working their way across and around it. The way the weeds held the house in a webbed grip made me think of the beautiful ultramarine glass orbs encased in netting ropes I saw in some of the fishing villages, which were used to secure floating nets but would occasionally untether themselves, drifting away for hundreds of miles, bobbing in the shallows before eventually washing up on distant shores neither cracked nor broken, gifted to foreign beaches as alien objects gleaming under the same one sun. Those that did shatter in the rolling wash, as with discarded ale and pop bottles, would have their jagged pieces smoothed away by the stones of the squall and the constant scrubbing of the salt water until they became the rounded glass treasures that are beloved of beachcombers and have filled many a childhood jar. For a long time I thought they were jewels that had drifted up from the jewel box of the seabed, and only became more fascinated with them when I learned they were the remnants of discarded everyday objects.

I decided I would search for some at the first available opportunity, but while I was inland I thought I might first investigate the badgers' lane that had inadvertently delivered me to Dulcie's.

Her house hunkered down there in the geologically dug green grave, crouched like an animal preparing for hibernation, and everywhere I turned on this hillside above were similar single stone houses with gardens and

outbuildings and barns and animal pens, each strate-
gically built to command an unimpeded sea view – all
except for Dulcie's house, where the untamed meadow
blocked the way, and which therefore seemed, like
Dulcie herself, to have little interest in what lay beyond
the perimeter of its vision.

I walked through one field and into the next. Rabbits
ran at our arrival, a dozen or more scattering in all
directions, the whites of their tails moving targets.

Butler barked and made a half-hearted attempt to
chase one, but experience seemed to tell him that they
could only be caught at close quarters or when stranded
out in the middle of an open pasture, and rabbits rarely
stray far from the safety of their shadowed sanctuar-
ies. Instead he looked at them with brief disdain, as if
the chasing of such common creatures – what we called
coney back at home – were beneath him.

Heading uphill and inland, the next field led to a
lower section of the holloway that I had walked in on.

Here I smelled something strong, and searched the
ground for a sign: there it was, off to one side, a pocked
patch of hollow holes where the soil was at its softest,
and in each was a stool, the colour of anthracite, some
coiled and others old and standing to attention, but all
with a sheen as if preserved beneath a shining lacquer.
The badgers' latrine, it was host to a smattering of
deposits polished deep in the innards of this indigenous
dawn-stalker as enduring and English as the single oak
tree or the scurrying hedgehog.

Butters trotted on, panting, and both of us wore a halo of flies about our hot heads.

Suddenly there was an explosion of movement up ahead as something crashed through a tight gap in the hedge, and a flash of rusted red blurred across the path. For a second I saw a deer, bounding up the near-vertical dirt bank like a convict up an escape ladder and into the copse that ran along beside us. Then it was gone. All that remained in its wake were a few falling leaves and the tiniest twist of fur snagged on a wire. I unhooked it and held it to the light, a rough knot of russet strands.

The lane was shaded and I sat for a while opposite the deep dug-out mounds of the badgers' sett. Behind them an impenetrable nettle patch provided good cover for further badger exits.

I stooped to the entrance of one of the holes and looked down into the cool portal that wound away beneath a tangle of overhanging roots, a helter-skelter slide into a nether world. Leaning in deeper, I pressed my head and shoulders into the hole. Badgers were nearby, docile and dormant. I could feel their presence as they no doubt could sense the proximity of an imposter crossing the single beam of light that penetrated their ancient ante-bunkers. I inhaled the smell of damp soil, of unseen England.

Further up, the sunken track ended abruptly where it met one of the back lanes, so I turned to face the sea once again and felt a tightening of excitement to see the full stretch of the coastal reach carving a craggy wall through the incandescent water, more expansive than ever.

I followed this rutted route for a while until I lost perspective, yawing far from any imagined directional line, then climbed over a stone wall and crossed a meadow that ran alongside a stream. The water was my guide, drawing me downhill, and I paused to let Butler lap at the slow-trickling rill before pushing through shrubs until I landed, stumbling and quite surprised, on the track that led back to Dulcie's hidden corner. Looking back, I had tracked an invisible circle across this hillside, and was grateful for the stone trough into which I dipped first my head and then my bare feet, one and then the other, the cold bite striking a note up through my legs and right to my very centre. I walked back barefoot, socks rolled into boots, boots in hand, head dripping water that tasted as fresh as the new season.

———

I worked all afternoon, hacking away at more of the stubborn weeds. I worked much longer than intended, locked into a rhythm of swinging and hacking, swinging and hacking, as the insects buzzed around me and the birds sang on, pausing only to drink great gulps of iced water flavoured with sugar and lemon, which Dulcie brought out for me.

As the day wore on, my hands, wrists, arms and bare torso became dotted with bramble nicks and scratches that looked like cryptic Morse code messages etched into my reddening skin. High afternoon became low-skulking evening and I stopped to survey the passage I had cleared through the grass, pleased at the headway I had made, though it still only represented the tiniest fraction of the meadow being tamed in any way. I did not trim the branches that obscured Dulcie's sea view.

Instead I walked deep down into the grass meadow and lay there for a few moments, listening to the thrum and rustle of it, and feeling the sun draw starburst patterns across my closed eyelids.

V

With only the thick lush grass around me and the sky above, I woke from a short deep nap. Shirtless, I lay confused for a few moments.

The past few weeks had been disorientating and not for the first time I briefly struggled to remember where I was exactly. Rarely had I done my ablutions in the same place twice, and I had long felt myself adrift from the binding timetable of school.

The dull strain of exhaustion and exertion ached in my back, shoulders and neck as I stood and slowly walked through the meadow back to the cottage to locate my pack. I was aware of my joints, and my skin felt stretched tight from the glare of the sun.

An evening dip in the sea was all I could think of and then, following that, perhaps some fish and chips and an early night in amongst a clifftop thicket, or in a rocky cove, perhaps, with a good fire going and nettle tea for company. I had a taste for it now.

There was no sign of Dulcie in the garden and when I knocked on the door of the cottage there was no reply, so I walked around to the back lane and peered in through the windows. I could see my backpack and blanket roll by the kitchen door. More framed photos hung in the narrow hallway alongside a wooden African mask and some mounted deer antlers. On a shelf I saw a clutch of peacock feathers in a vase and a cluster of shells and pebbles, and beneath it a large cushion covered in coarse dog hairs that Butler slept on.

I returned to the garden and sat down in a chair to wait for her. My eyes felt heavy again.

Then Dulcie was standing there in her wide-brimmed hat, a silent silhouette with the sun behind her and a glass in each hand.

'You have the leathered look of a proper land worker,' she said. 'You wear it well.'

I rubbed my eyes and stretched, squinting into the late-afternoon glare.

'Cocktail time,' she said.

'I'm afraid I'm not quite finished. There's still some clearing-up to do.'

She held out a glass to me. 'Cocktail time.'

The drink within was light red in colour and there were cubes of apple floating in it, and ice and strawberries too.

'I know what you're thinking,' Dulcie said as I took it from her.

'You do?'

'Yes. But I froze a batch last year, you see, for just such occasions.' If Dulcie could read my mind, then evidently she saw that it was empty, for she continued: 'The strawberries. Even with this warm spell it's too early.'

I took a sip of the drink and it fizzed with new flavours in my mouth, sweet and sharp.

'That's smashing, that is. What's in it?'

'A bit of everything in the cupboard and then some.'

'I thought I'd just finish off the last bit of the trimming, tidy up, and then I should probably get going.'

'Now?'

'Well, soon, yes.'

'Aren't you exhausted after all that labour?'

'A little. I had a nap and I can walk off the aches, I'm sure. Or perhaps an evening swim.'

'There are the tides to consider and' – Dulcie nodded to a basket slung over one arm – 'I've just been to get tea.'

'Oh, there's really no need.'

'There's never a *need*.'

'I've only just paid off breakfast and that lovely lunch.'

Dulcie studied my face for a moment.

'Regardless, you still need to eat. And I'm not going through this ridiculous bartering rigmarole again, as earnest as your intentions may be.'

'I had thought maybe fish and chips.'

'Then you thought correctly, because that's precisely what we're having.'

I sipped my drink and chewed on an ice cube.

'You're being too kind.'

'It's a bit of fish and some chipped potatoes, Robert, and one can never be too kind. Unless of course you're desperate to flee the grip of this old crone, in which case flee, flee to the horizon, I won't be remotely offended, nor will Butler who will find his dog bowl rather full tonight. Though it does seem he's rather taken to you, haven't you – ' She looked around. 'Where *has* that beast got to?'

Searching for the dog, Dulcie removed her hat, which was as large as a sombrero, dabbed at her brow with a handkerchief and then replaced it.

'I'll batter it.'

'The dog?'

Dulcie snorted, whooping with laughter. 'The fish. The fish, you stiff plum. I have a John Dory that's as long as my forearm and as ugly as a pug that's done twelve rounds with Max Schmeling, but it'll be as tasty as you like. Barton brought it up.'

I took another big swig of the drink.

'Look,' said Dulcie, 'let me put a fish in you, then you can be on your way. An army marches on its belly and though you're a sole soldier gone rogue you still need refuelling. The horizon awaits. Eat, then go to greet it.'

'Remind me how old you are again, Robert.'

The perfectly preserved backbones of the filleted fish lay stripped of skin and flesh. I watched as a bluebottle landed on its dorsal fin, joined a moment later by a second one. What we could not consume was theirs for the picking.

'I'm sixteen.'

Dulcie's eyes widened. 'I knew you were young, but that's obscene. *Sixteen*.'

I laughed. 'Is it?'

'Yes. Sixteen is barely even a memory for me. Sixteen is a foreign country. Sixteen is a photograph in a suitcase left on a train bound for the Orient long ago. Some might suggest that to have so much ahead of you is utterly enviable, though if I had a chance to do it again I wouldn't. At least not now.'

'Why not?'

'Well, I hate to be the drop of pessimism in the unspoiled pool of youthful purity, but more war seems an inevitability. Just more male horseshit. Trust me, I resent the fact I've been forced to take this stance – it's against my nature – but at least a pessimist is rarely disappointed with life. That's pragmatism, something else I've come to quite late.'

'I'm just thinking day to day,' I said, and I meant it, for to contemplate the life that awaited me at home – six days a week at the colliery then tending to a hangover and the allotment leeks on a Sunday – or indeed what might lie ahead in the future for the wider world, left me feeling deflated within seconds.

'A capital attitude. Let's pretend tomorrow may never appear.'

'It did yesterday,' I quipped.

'Oh, very good,' she said. 'Then let's ditch the diary, burn the calendar, smash the clocks and instead pretend that today is infinite, and punctuated only by the darkening of the sky and the hooting of the owl. What I mean is, let's cock a snook to time, for time is just another set of self-imposed arbitrary boundaries designed to capture and control. Let today run forever, Robert. Do you see what we're doing here? We're subverting the very thing that holds humanity together. We're shaking off the chains. Isn't it brilliant?'

Between us Dulcie and I had drunk another cocktail and the better part of another bottle of white wine and I felt loose and liquid of limb as I slouched in the chair, sliding ever closer to a horizontal position. The day was defeating me and I was happy to put up little resistance. But Dulcie was in full flow, an unstoppable deluge of words brought in on the tide of the mind.

'Do you know,' she continued, 'I've been up to your neck of the woods. To the university, for a conference. I saw that horse of yours.'

'I don't have a horse.'

'Of course you do: the one that stands in the market-place.'

'Oh,' I replied. 'You must mean the statue.'

'It's quite remarkable, isn't it?'

'Is it?'

I didn't go into the city much at all; that would require a bus journey in from the village and a bus journey required money, and I never had any. I had only visited the cathedral once, on a school trip. The city seemed to me a place for lecturers and students in their gowns and silly hats, and young men and women who went to the good schools and carried stacks of books beneath their arms, and who didn't speak as I spoke, and who would soon join the academics and students at their seats of higher learning in other such cities. It was a place where clergymen dashed down cobbled streets and coxes shouted orders through loudhailers at the rowing crews who trained on the river, and tourists alighted from charabancs to stand and point at the castle, and people ate scones and drank pots of tea from chiming china cups and saucers while sitting in pretty Georgian windows, and flush-faced rugby teams celebrated their latest successes on the playing fields with pub crawls.

The only real reason to visit was for the Miners' Gala, which we called the Big Meeting, for one Saturday in July, when all the colliery bands would gather to march and play, and we would carry the banners all the way down to the racecourse fields, where there were speeches and stalls and fairground rides, and tens of thousands of people would eat and drink and sing, and gypsy boys would strip off their tops to fight the local boys, and evening would turn to night and we'd take the long ride home, our stomachs sick with sugar and too many chips. But that was for one day a year, and I had not been since I was a child, because for the six long years of the war the Miners' Gala had been cancelled, and this year I would miss it anyway. It seemed as if Dulcie knew my home city better than I did.

'The horse is remarkable for a number of reasons, not least because it is green,' she continued. 'I've been around the world many times but I have never seen a green horse. I've seen one you could fit in a medium-sized suitcase, and one twice the height of a man, and I've seen hundreds of sea horses, and once rode a horse entirely Godiva-like for a bet, but I have never seen a green one cast in electroplated copper and buffed by hundreds of years of rain that has fallen from the sky of time like rusty daggers. In this instance the colour of the horse is not even the most remarkable thing about it. That honour belongs to the story that has followed it around like an immortal horsefly that, no matter how many times it is swatted by a swish of a copper tail, somehow always remains. I shall tell you it now.

'Once there was a man called Raffaelle Monti. He was an Italian artist, a sculptor, born and raised in Milan, who by the 1850s had been living in England for some time. I think maybe love led him here, though I can't be sure. This story is a jigsaw and some of the pieces marked "fact" are missing, so I'm fashioning a few new ones of my own. Anyway, this Monti chap was commissioned to sculpt a big horse to take pride of place in your market square, to commemorate something or another – a great but pointless battle, no doubt. The townsfolk had one stipulation: there had to be someone riding the horse and the figure was to be some wealthy nobleman. "I'll build you a green horse," said Monti. "A fucking great big one." And he did. He built a big horse that was elegant and accurate and spellbindingly horselike. Its size and its greenness were just two of the more obvious reasons why it was a horse to start a thousand conversations. On his back rode the Marquis of Whoever, an equally elegant and accurate rendering. In 1861 the sculpture was completed and officially unveiled in the marketplace. "This horse is perfect," Monti announced. "Perfect in all ways." "It's green," said a little boy. "It's still perfect," replied the great sculptor. "Furthermore, if anyone can find a single anatomical fault with this horse and his noble rider, then I shall be shamed into suicide. For this is no mere work of art, this is a dream cast in iron, mounted on stone and placed where all will see it for hundreds of years to come."'

Dulcie paused and took a sip of her drink. She was taking her time with the story. Relishing it.

'Well. With such a challenge issued, the townsfolk were soon climbing the scaffolding in order to examine the horse for themselves, while Monti just stood to one side, arms folded, sucking on a lollipop for he had recently attempted to give up smoking again. And he was right: there were no faults to be found with this great green creature that was the crowning glory of the town. Time passed. A number of weeks, maybe months. People still liked to stop and check on the horse. It had become something of a tradition for many people, as if it were on their shopping lists: *go into town, buy parsnips and bread, check big green horse for anatomical inaccuracies.* One day a blind man appeared and said that he would like to inspect the horse with his highly sensitive fingers. He was soon given permission and a helping hand up there. A small crowd gathered as he felt his way around the horse – its smooth underbelly and thick copper mane, its flared glorious nostrils. The crowd were getting restless. Finally the blind man climbed down and announced his verdict. "This horse has no tongue," he said, then turned and went home. "It has no tongue!" said the locals, who had hung around, the first faint smell of blood filling their twitching nostrils. "The horse has no tongue – quick, somebody get Raffaelle Monti." They were excited now. "He owes us a suicide," one fellow was heard to remark. The sculptor was alerted to this development. He was not pleased – he had just accepted another commission in his home city of Milan. But a deal was a deal. Raffaelle Monti proceeded straight to the cathedral. Once there he ascended the three hundred and twenty-five steps up to the highest tower, then, as a crowd gathered below, threw himself off the top to a not-entirely-instant death below.'

'That's awful,' I said.

'Well, that would have been the end of the story but for one small thing,' said Dulcie. 'The horse *did* have a tongue. In their excitement, no one had thought to verify the blind man's findings, least of all poor Raffaelle Monti, who in his artistically exhausted state was not thinking straight. He had been lost in the certainty of his craftsmanship. The horse had a tongue but the people refused to believe it. They had wanted imperfection so badly. The massive green horse *was* perfect after all, but it was too late for that. A myth was already forming, a story to be passed on, an heirloom to store in the attic of the mind. And as you know, there the statue sits today, noble and unmoving amongst the turbulence of the world around it. You yourself must have seen people sitting at the base of the sculpture, perhaps wiling away a few minutes as they think about the past, the present and maybe the future too. But sooner or later they all get up, brush down the seat of their trousers and wander off, yawning and checking the sky for the threat of incoming thunder like the hooves of a horse bigger than any dream or sculpture can imagine.'

'Is that really all true?' I wondered.

Dulcie first frowned at me, and then smiled, but she said nothing.

———

Beneath the table Butler finished off a fistful of twice-fried chips, the best I had ever tasted, and then gently nudged my knee for more. I drifted out of another of Dulcie's meandering monologues, though she did not appear to notice and carried on talking, her train of thought a slow-moving river gliding through the flatlands of the evening's landscape. I fed the dog another chip that was dripping in vinegar the colour of a dozen drops of blood in a beaker of salt water.

'But then what follows?'

Dulcie's question stirred me from my wine-and-carbohydrate reverie. I lifted my head, my smile sloppy. 'Sorry, I was just – '

'What I mean to say is, do you have any inclination as to what else you might *do* with your life?'

'*Do?*'

'Yes, do. Beyond this Homeric voyage.'

'I'm not entirely sure,' I said.

'That's not necessarily a bad thing. Any young man who has his life planned is to be pitied, as plans rarely leave room for happenstance or serendipity, and furthermore each man – if he is man at all – is an ever-changing entity himself, as too is the world around him. What blighted lives those burdened by familial expectation or tradition lead.'

'I think I'd like to be flexible. Maybe I could fly planes, like Douglas Bader.'

'An interesting point about this new national hero of ours,' Dulcie replied. 'Did you know that he actually had his legs replaced by tin ones after he crashed his plane while messing about above a training ground? War and Bader's capture in France in 1941 had nothing to do with it; at this point the Third Reich was little more than one madman's pipe dream. The heroism lay in the fact that he was later brave or suicidal enough to fly with tin pins. Personally, I think it's asking for trouble. I've also heard that he happens to be something of a git. But I digress. In my experience, those whose careers are predestined turn out to be fatuous bores. These are the men who become our bank managers, financiers and politicians power-drunk on their own sense of entitlement. The ignoble ones. Their palettes are dull, their imaginations stunted. They shrink their worlds down to nothing, you know, Robert, they really do. The 5:42 from Waterloo each evening back to the house in the shires, and the quiet desperation of a connubial marriage crumbling. No, thank you, matey. No, *thank you*.'

'In a way it's not that different to me and my father and his father and his father's father, what with them all going down the pit,' I said.

'You must feel the burden of expectation like a sack of the black stuff on your back, then.'

I shrugged. 'I'll expect my dad will try to set me on soon enough.'

'Presumably it's a profession fraught with danger.'

'It can be. But it's not all bad. The pit looks after you. The wages are good, and there's the baths and the library and the club and all of that. Houses too, for those that want to start a family.'

Dulcie emptied the last of the wine she had decanted into a carafe that appeared never to leave the table, then took a drink.

'Have you considered higher education?'

'Like university?'

'Exactly like university.'

I scratched the dog behind his ears and took more wine.

'People like me don't go to places like that.'

'What do you mean by "people like me"?'

'Coal folk.'

'But you've got a working organ in your brainpan, haven't you?'

'I hope so.'

'You clearly have. And that's all you need.'

I smiled. 'And the rest.'

'However do you mean?'

'You need the right clothes and the right way of talking, for starters.'

Dulcie tutted. 'Complete nonsense. You can hold your own, I'm sure. All you need is an appetite to learn and if it matches your appetite for food I imagine there's no shortage.'

I felt my cheeks redden at the possible embarrassment of being seen as gluttonous.

'Do you read much?'

'Sometimes,' I replied. 'We've not many books in our house.'

'What do you enjoy?'

'I liked comics for a while but that seems like kiddies' stuff now. I like adventure stories.'

'Like what?'

I racked my brain. '*The Thirty-Nine Steps* was fantastic.'

'Yes, Buchan. My father knew him.'

'Your father knew the man who wrote *The Thirty-Nine Steps*?'

'As I recall, he lent him money.'

'Was he a writer too, your dad?'

'Heavens, no, though he was good at writing cheques for mistresses. No, he knew Buchan in Canada. How did you get on with school?'

I shrugged. 'I'd rather have been outside.'

'And now you are, so you're already on top of things. Did they teach you much poetry at all?'

'They made us read Shakespeare.'

'The sonnets?'

'*Romeo and Juliet*, I think it was.'

Dulcie screwed up her face. 'That's not poetry,' she said. 'That's archaic drama, written to be performed on theatre stages, not read aloud in stuffy classrooms. Presented incorrectly and out of context it will put you off for life, but a good poem shucks the oyster shell of one's mind to reveal the pearl within. It gives words to those feelings whose definitions are forever beyond the reach of verbal articulation. Bill Shakey has his moments.'

'The bits they made us read were boring. It made no sense to me. It was like a foreign language.'

Dulcie gestured by prodding her glass towards me, slopping some wine on her wrist. 'Then they were making you read the wrong ones. The wrong ones, I say. And that's nothing short of a tragedy in itself. What you need is poetry you can relate to.'

'I doubt there is any.'

'My dear boy, of course there is. *Of course* there is. Trust me when I say that everything you've ever felt has been experienced by another human being before you. You may not think so, but it's true. That is what poetry is. It exists to remind us of this very fact. Poetry is mankind's way of saying that we are not entirely alone in the world; it offers a voice of comfort to resonate down through the ages like a lone foghorn's mournful call in the nautical night. Poetry is a stepladder between the centuries, from ancient Greece to tomorrow afternoon. Your problem is you just haven't been introduced to the pure poets – those who hit the head and the heart. The masters. But luckily for you, you have pitched at the right place. I'd say it is almost as if it were fate, if I could bring myself to believe in such an ethereal concept. Now: you're a young man who has a romantic head on his shoulders, am I right?'

'I'm not much into soppy stuff,' I said, 'no.'

'And I didn't say you were. Romance needn't mean love hearts and red roses, you know. Romance is feelings and romance is freedom. Romance is adventure and nature and wanderlust. It is the sound of the sea and the rain on your tarpaulin and a buzzard hovering across the meadow and waking in the morning to wonder what the day will bring and then going to find out. *That* is romance.'

'Well, if you put it like that,' I said, 'then yes, perhaps I am a bit romantic. I'd never really thought about it.'

'So you need to read some like-minded souls. Here – wait a minute. I'll see what I can find.'

Dulcie stood and went into the house. The dog rose with her and went to follow but settled back down when she told him to stay. He lay beside her empty chair and glanced up at me twice and then sighed and lowered his chin to his outstretched oversized paws. I heard her feet on the stairs and then a thudding sound of books being moved and dropped. She reappeared with an armful of tomes and tipped them onto the table.

'What about Lawrence?' she asked. 'You've heard of *Chatterley*, I expect?'

I adjusted myself in the chair. 'Yes,' I said, and then, realising that there was no point pretending, I said more quietly: 'I mean, no.'

'You really must read him. In fact, I shall keep you hostage until you do. I think a young man like you with blood in his veins and desire in his stones might take to him, though you'd be hard-pushed to get an unex-purgated copy like mine. This is writing that is full of the fecundity of life. At his best he pulses. The animal within and the world without, that is what Lawrence writes best about.'

I must have pulled a face at this. Aware that I was confused, Dulcie elaborated.

'*Sex*,' she said. 'Sex, and the poetry of it all. Indoor sports and outdoor gymnastics; he was obsessed, as many of the best minds are. In places his prose is prac-tically *tumescent*. Of course they punished him for it.'

My cheeks flushed with prickly heat, yet I wanted to know more. 'Punished him – how?'

'Didn't you hear? They charged him first with obscenity then for spying in the Great War. Ridiculous. The only thing Bert spied on was shirtless farmhands and cuckoos' nests. But they drove him abroad all the same, the publishers, the critics and puritans. Too many fucks and cunts for their liking, I expect, but to me that was missing the point.'

The remainder of my wine caught in my throat and I covered my mouth with my hand, spluttering droplets into it. Beneath the table I discreetly wiped my palm on my trousers, as Dulcie carried on regardless.

'Hasn't history shown us that visionaries are rarely welcomed in their home countries, and so very often exiled?' she said. 'And he was such a *nice* boy, really. He only ever swore on the page, that's the irony of it. Here – '

I turned the book over in my hand. It was *Women in Love.* In blue ink the book was inscribed to Dulcie.

'Did you know him too?' I asked.

'I met him in New Mexico on more than one occasion when we were out there. He wasn't hard to miss: auburn hair and skin the colour of mouldy flour. A beard in the heat. Very English. The whitest gringo on the continent, I'd say. Charming, though, and interested in everything. I called him Bert, after his middle name – Herbert. Frieda was a dear too, a friend of a friend. She was his wife. Another German. Actually, to merely call her "his wife" is to fall foul of man's propensity to perpetually diminish the role of women: she was so much more. She was his patron, his muse, his lover, his salvation. The glue that held his bones together. She sacrificed a lot so that he might write – her own children, some have said. A formidable lady, Frieda. Our paths crossed several times after that, but that's another story for another day. The tragedy of it all is, I doubt Bert could get arrested today even if he ran through Eastwood starkers.'

'Are you still in touch?'

'Not unless I go to New Mexico and dig up his yellow bones. Tuberculosis took him some time back. Even then the obituaries were hostile. These castrated critics somehow resented him for contriving to be decades ahead of his time. Yes, Bert was the best of men, though I take solace in the knowledge that the world will catch up one day.'

Dulcie shook her head, then continued.

'And that is why it is the responsibility of people like me to spread the good gospel to people like you, Robert, the next generation. The best minds are too often reviled, and complacency about such matters spawns little except mediocrity, but between us, the likes of you and I, we must fight to make the world a more liveable, colourful and exciting place. Lord knows it's needed now more than ever. No one starts wars when they are fulfilled, that much is certain, and the pursuit of personal freedom can now be viewed as a radical act. And that is my point, Robert. You must live your life exactly how you wish to, not for anyone else. We are on the cusp of great changes, trust me. All innocence is gone, so now what? Freedom, and the pursuit of it: that's what we must strive for at all times. The future may be uncertain but it is yours for the taking. Something good has to come out of all this senseless violence. Let poetry and music and wine and romance guide the way. Let liberty prevail. Here – try this for size.'

Dulcie handed me another book. I read the spine. Lawrence again: *Lady Chatterley's Lover.*

'It's as rare as rocking-horse dung, that edition. Thoroughly banned.'

'Have you met lots of famous people, Dulcie?' I wondered.

'Over the years, yes, I suppose I have.'

'Are you famous?'

'No, thank God.' Her face darkened. 'I've seen enough of it at close quarters to know that fame, renown, notoriety – call it what you will – well, it's nothing but a curse that breeds misery. Especially to those of a creative or artistic bent. For many years I have observed that the truly talented are invariably the most sensitive, and the public arena, where artifice is all that really matters, is no place for poets, and furthermore the critics, most of whom don't know their bumholes from their earlobes when it comes to the written word, think everyone – private life and all – is fair game. Yes, the public arena is no place for those of, shall we say, a sensitive disposition. No poet should be famous – only read.'

I looked at the book again. 'Did D. H. Lawrence give you this copy?'

'Actually a suitor bought me a rare uncensored edition when it sneaked out in '32. Perhaps he had designs on being the Mellors to my Lady. It got him nowhere, though. For all the brouhaha, the book is not even about mindless rutting anyway, not really; it's about class, and this fellow had very little of it, because if he *had* he would have taken the trouble to get to know me first, and then he might have found out a few things that would have turned his chubby cheeks puce. I suggest you read Bert's poems too.' Here she handed me a slim volume. 'Yes, it's a pungent England that he describes. A fertile place teeming with life, as I imagine some parts of it out there still are, beneath the grime and the growling bellies.'

Dulcie rifled through the other books.

'Now. What else. Well, Whitman. *Leaves of Grass*, of course, for an American perspective. A big influence on Lawrence, and many others. There's Shelley. John Clare. Robinson Jeffers – another septic.'

'Septic?'

'Yes, a Sherman. A tank.' Dulcie smiled. 'A Yank, Robert.'

'Oh.'

'An interesting chap, Jeffers; worshipped across the water but little-known here. Also Auden, Keats. You should probably investigate some of the young boys on the other war too, but I suspect it's the last thing you want just now. And I can't give you works entirely by men, can I? So we must also turn to Emily Dickinson, Christina Rossetti and – for a bit of northern gritstone – Emily Brontë too. The Heathcliff story is worth a dabble, though it needs a bloody good editor.'

She pushed a small pile of books towards me.

'Have what you want.'

'Thank you. I'll look after them.'

'Take them, take them,' said Dulcie. 'It's good to have a purgation. It's not the books that really matter anyway, Robert. Books are just paper, but they contain within them revolutions. You'll find that most dictators barely read beyond their own grubby hagiographies. That's where they're going wrong: not enough poetry in their lives.'

It was a close evening and the sky was starting to moil. Clouds clustered and tumbled, eating themselves. The warmth of earlier had grown into a damp, cloying heat and there was a tightening of the air that matched a dull pain down one side of my neck that was threatening to spread into a headache. I stood and stepped up onto my chair to get a better view of the sea, where a foreshadowing curtain was being drawn across the water. Between the low-scudding rain clouds and the sea there was a mottled movement, a shifting shape like a swarm of insects, but which was in fact columns of sea-born rain coalescing and then separating again as they blew in on the cooler winds of the northern continent. It was as if the sea itself were being sucked up skywards.

The rain was many miles out, yet here in the garden it had fallen suddenly still and noticeably silent. No birds were calling. No distant dog barked. The muscle in my neck throbbed with an almost electric pulse.

Butler raised his gaze again.

'They call it the offing,' said Dulcie, quietly.

I climbed down from the chair. She gestured down the meadow.

'That distant stretch of sea where sky and water merge. It's called the offing.'

'I didn't know that.'

'Know something else: I wouldn't risk a ramble with that roarer rolling in. But then I am not you, am I? If I were I'd probably feel like I'd had my ear bent and been burdened with books, which, now that I stop and consider it, will be impossible for you to carry on your epic voyage. What am I thinking?'

The sky rumbled. The dog's ears pricked up: two furry sound mirrors pointed out to sea, tuned to the changing atmosphere.

The first full drops of rain fell then.

Dulcie said, 'Might as well uncork another bottle and watch the show.'

VI

Plumb-line rain fell that night. Elongated drops as straight and true as stair rods. It fell so heavily that I hastily moved my camp into the shack. I barged the jammed door open and once settled was more than happy to share the space with the rats or whatever rodents seemed to skitter in the crawl space beneath the creaking floorboards.

The wind lifted and then dropped and then lifted again, and a flat malevolent whistle shrieked around the corner of the cabin.

The downpour played an urgent marching-band beat on the old moss-covered corrugated roof, first building to a chaotic symphony of thunderous rhythms, and then as it slowed again I heard a trickle from the drainpipe by the back corner, broken halfway down, and the patter of droplets in the peat-coloured puddle that gathered below it.

I tried to read one of Dulcie's books by candlelight, but a draught that penetrated the shack blew the flames near-horizontal and, parched from a day of too much sun and wine, I instead took sips of rainwater from a tin cup that I filled from the drainpipe.

I awoke once in the deepest part of the night to the sound of snorting and something of a reasonable size rubbing up against the shed, but I did not stir, and instead lay in my sleeping bag as still as a bandaged mummy, and listened as its footsteps retreated, rustling off through the long grass.

By early morning the storm had abated to slacken the sky's tension. The ashen sea roared in the distance like a football stadium witnessing an extra-time injustice, a turbulent commotion that echoed up the hillside. From the grimy window of the shack I could just see out beyond the bay, across to the ragged promontory three or four miles south. Here lay the remains of a philanthropist's long-abandoned attempt to build a clifftop spa resort. All that was left were the unused sewers, the markings of streets never built and a large solitary hotel perched high atop a cliff too vertical for the sea ever to be easily reachable for its residents. The building was a dark speck in the distance, just one more imaginative man's doomed end-of-empire folly.

The sun rose lazily over the meadow, pale and wan at first, but then gaining in strength and luminescent power, and as it began to blaze a golden morning across the streaming meadow, a deer appeared in the overgrown edges to sniff the warming air.

It took several steps forward on legs that looked impossibly thin, stood for a few long moments during which I dared not move, even at some distance away in the shack. Evidently it heard something imperceptible for it turned tail and ran into the trees, but I stayed unmoving, my unwashed face reflected in the mottled glass.

A fug of flying insects gathered as bees and wasps and moths and butterflies and dragonflies took flight. I carried my sleeping bag outside and shook away the dust of decades.

Breakfast was light: a boiled egg and an apple each, plus nettle tea.

'The second-best thing for hangovers, after another dash of the sauce that got you sick in the first place,' explained Dulcie. 'But seeing as this is low-level, the eggs should do it. Protein.'

We drank more tea and I felt myself coming back to life.

'Did you sleep?'

'Very well.'

'I expect you'll be on your way, then.'

'Yes,' I said. 'I'll just clear away yesterday's trimmings. I'm sure I've stayed long enough.'

We sat silently finishing our breakfast, and then Dulcie spoke.

'That wasn't a hint. If I had tired of your company you'd know about it. Life is too short for hints. Plain speaking and direct action, those are my favoured modes of communication. Those who are easily offended are surely not worth knowing for any length of time. Would you agree?'

Again, I wasn't sure what I thought so I just nodded, and thought about how so many people I knew back in the village preferred to say nothing rather than suffer the embarrassment of speaking the truth. Only in these passive silences was the truth to be found.

A final half-hour of toil passed as I raked grass trimmings and pulled a passage of weeds and wild grass, stopping only when I noticed that my wrists and forearms had come up with a rash of white welts and red, irritated skin. I walked back to the cottage, scratching away at them. Dulcie saw me.

'Let me see.'

I held out my arms to her. She shook her head.

'I'd wager hogweed. Nasty business, but you're lucky. People can go blind.'

'Really?'

'Really. *Heracleum mantegazzianum*: hogweed of the giant variety. It can burn like billy-o, by all accounts. An invasive, pugnacious bugger. Come, that needs rinsing before it blisters or scars. Soap and cold water, straight away.'

She led me to an outside spout and turned it on, just as my skin was beginning to feel like it was burning. Dulcie fetched a bar of soap and I got a good lather going. When I finished, my wrists and forearms looked redder than before, and my hands were slightly swollen, as if they had been struck by hammers.

Tutting, Dulcie turned them one way and then the other.

'I'll apply a poultice, just to be safe.'

'It's fine, really. It's just a bit of a reaction.'

Soon I had rolled away my blankets and tarpaulin, and had my kitbag ready. I was torn between resting a while longer, or at least until the scorched sensation that was spreading up my arms abated, and heading off before the lazier hours of afternoon beckoned and my departure would surely be further delayed.

I bent down and scratched behind the dog's large ears one more time. They felt warm in my hand, like hot flannels from a radiator.

'Thank you for feeding me,' I said to Dulcie. 'It's beautiful here.'

Distractedly, she watched a butterfly alight upon a leaf.

'It's a different world come winter.'

'I bet.'

'Stop by again if you're passing. Butters would love to see you again, I'm sure.'

The dog looked up at me.

'Oh, I nearly forgot.'

She went into the cottage and then returned with a small brown paper package.

'What is it?'

'A dried sausage. Or rather a string of them. German. They call them *Landjäger*; they keep for months. Years, even. Cast your preconceptions aside and enjoy something to nibble on. I thought it might change your mind about our Teutonic cousins.'

'Where did you get them from?'

Dulcie didn't reply. Instead she simply said, 'Goodbye, Robert', and walked into the house. I was left standing in a silence that seemed to hang heavy with things unsaid and was, perhaps, beneath it all tinged with the faintest streak of regret.

The dog followed me to the end of the lane, and then he too turned back.

Above the bay, grand houses looked out as the sun threw copper shards of shrapnel shapes across the silk sheet of the sea.

Many of their gardens had been turned over and kept as vegetable patches, and several held chicken coops. One even had a pigpen and a run for the hogs, who grunted excitedly as they pressed themselves up against the fence when I passed. Further on there was a postal office, a general store and a row of guest houses, each with a VACANCIES sign in its window. I caught glimpses into neat parlours where everything was polished, buffed and ordered; rooms that held little-used tea services, armchairs forever covered with protective sheeting, parted crinoline nets like wisps of cloud that were washed twice monthly, and slothful cats overfed on the breakfast-plate scrapings of fried bread crusts, sausage nubs and grey strings of bacon rind, stretching and yawning from their afternoon-windowsill suntraps.

My wrists and forearms felt more inflamed than ever and as I walked I scratched at them to little satisfaction.

At the end of the row, positioned so that the curved windows of the dining room appeared to perch on the cliff edge like the prow of a pioneer's galleon cutting through the vast unknown of waters not yet mapped, framing a panorama of the sea as it broadened out vertiginously, was an old red-brick hotel. The menu outside was held fast beneath glass and partly obscured by a greasy streak of seagull shit, and offered a mouth-watering selection that I could never hope to afford.

I couldn't help but contemplate the meals that Dulcie made, and how much they might cost in such a restaurant were its chef even capable of sourcing the ingredients that she seemed to miraculously get her hands upon. My stomach growled a little as I thought of her wonderfully cluttered kitchen, and then the road ahead.

The challenge of feeding myself from very little required both effort and imagination and sat before me like a giant question mark blocking the sun upon awaking each morning. And now that an insatiable appetite had been awakened, enlivened, briefly cultivated and almost certainly indulged, that challenge no longer felt quite as thrilling.

More than that was the unshakeable thought that Dulcie had seen me in a way entirely unprejudiced by familiarity, history or expectation. That is, she had taken me as she found me, and not only that, but had seen fit to treat me as someone worth bothering with – not quite an equal, for it was clear that she was a wise, worldly and original person and I was none of these. Yet in our brief time together I had begun to feel as if I was becoming someone else. I was approaching being myself, rather than the person I had been living as. Dulcie had seen me as I was, and not been bored or uninterested.

Yet still a stubbornness and an emerging sense of the curious self drove me away from Dulcie and her full larder and into an unknown future. As the road dropped downwards and my knees took the strain, I descended into a huddled cluster of streets of old fishermen's cottages much smaller than the opulent Victorian abodes up top.

Closely packed and with barely a straight vertical or horizontal line in sight, the squat homes of the lower bay were separated by wonky ginnels down which there were more cottages so close that their inhabitants could reach across from one dim living room to another. It was a cobbled, disorientating place of shadows, angles and caliginous corners pierced by sudden slits of morning sunlight penetrating the gaps between buildings; of small windows and steep slick steps that led down to gloomy cellars and secret passages once used for smuggling. It was said that stolen barrels of liquor could be transferred from the sea to the top of the village, and then off onto England's black market, without ever seeing daylight. I was, as they say, down bay.

Out the front of these houses were old handmade lobster creels in various states of repair, coils of fraying rope, plant pots in which there grew herbs such as parsley, chives and thyme, pieces of driftwood sea-worn into weathered abstract lengths and lumps, and everywhere I turned there were more hand-blown glass floats, coloured pieces of glass shining in the sun, and stones through which there ran the patterned veins of prehistoric substrata or fossils of strange creatures from a time when all was cooling larval rock and sinking sediment. Stones whose pictures I had pored over in my lunch hour in the school library during dank and unforgiving days.

Strung between the houses were lines of drying items – children's knitwear, rubber waders, sopping ganseys – or colourful clippy mats ready to have the dust beaten out of them, and below them galoshes upturned on wrought-iron racks. Out of curiosity I took one such alley, drawn perhaps by the lingering stench of kippers split and hung from racks in a smokehouse at the far edge of the village's limit, before turning a corner and finding myself back on the road that led down to the narrowing jumble of the lower bay.

I passed several stout but not unfriendly locals, many of them women carrying baskets in the crooks of their arms, others passing time in idle conversation from which they paused to offer a greeting to this passing stranger who was a rare sight on a weekday before full summer had taken hold.

The road wound down, steep and curious. A fishmonger's window held the catch of the day, while the greengrocer's seemed rather bereft of anything green. At a bakery I bought two large, fresh floured rolls. I counted three snug pubs before the road ended abruptly at a stone slipway from which the fishing boats were launched daily and then hauled back up once again upon their return.

On the beach below, the tide had deposited large tangled banks of seaweed, gluey and bubbling, and receded enough to reveal the wooden groynes planted to create a corridor through which generations of boats had navigated a passage. Limpets and barnacles clung decoratively to the wet rocks, and fleshy red anemones too, so beautiful when submerged and in full bloom but deflated and melancholy looking gelatinous blobs when stranded at low tide.

I walked across sandbanks dotted with spiralling piles of lugworm residue as the sea receded to further reveal stone scaurs. I walked over shifting sheaves of bladderwrack, sea lettuce and red kelp that lay splayed across the rutted sands, patiently awaiting the next tidal turn to bring it back to life as a string puppet awaits the return of its master.

Along the beach the cliffs were in a perpetual state of reshaping, where chimneys and scarps and shelves periodically fell crumbling, and where time was marked not by years or decades or centuries, but by the re-emergence of those species trapped in the clay here: the ammonites, haematites and bracken fronds pressed flat between the pages of past epochs. Each was a book-mark placed in Britain's ongoing story, and the land itself was a sculpture, a work in progress.

I looked out across the water as it rose in gentle berms and then curled and broke in waves of hissing white spume, shifting the shale beneath in a hypnotic percussive rattle of stone on stone.

The sea was an hourglass tipped and then tipped again with each turning tide. As I ascended at a sharp angle, overhead a gull offered a greeting.

I ate my roll and then stripped to my shorts and ran down to the water, hurling myself into the sea to cool my prickling skin and finally enjoy the first fully submerged wash in weeks.

The seabed was a jagged morass of pebbles and smashed shells swirling around my ankles. The water made my bones feel forged, indestructible, and as the brown brine turned to a fizzing foam a larger wave, the seventh in a set, took me by surprise and though I turned my back to it at the last moment and was still only chest-deep it walloped my neck, defiantly slapped my face, filled one ear to deafness and sent me stumbling into the gelid squall.

But the tentative totter of warm blood entering cold waters was over. My heart was below the waterline and my neck, the nerve centre through which all the body's sensory messages pass, was wet too, so I pushed off and let the North Sea take my weight, my feet kicking a dark void as I swam out, each rising wave rising through me, lifting me up, the force of the moon exerting itself as the land disappeared from view between each undulation, everything on it obscured.

Soon my body was warm and I felt deliriously alive. The salt water soothed the hogweed burns and I floated on my back, thinking of nothing.

At the slipway a fisherman was tending to a knotted coil of blue rope as thick as my wrist. Beside him were a stack of creels and four baskets containing the best of that morning's haul.

'You'd not catch me in there,' he said, rolling up the sleeves of his gansey as I passed.

I smiled. 'It's not so bad once you're in. Refreshing.'

He sniffed. 'Fishermen don't swim.'

'Why not?'

'Most can't. Still, there's worse days for it, I suppose.'

He stooped and lifted from his basket a couple of mackerel. 'Here you are. For the old dear.'

He said this not as a question, but a statement.

'For – ?'

'For Dulcie.'

For a moment I was confused as to how he knew who I was.

'You *are* the lad that's been stopping up there.'

'Aye. But – '

'Well, you'll save me the bother if you can fetch them back with you. I said I'd send something her way but I've got errands to run and these creels to fix. Best kept fresh if they're not straight off to the smokehouse, are mackerel.'

'You must be Mr Barton.'

He nodded. 'Aye.'

'Your lobster was smashing.'

'Give it a month when they've fattened up and we're in full season, then you'll know what smashing is.'

'That's what Dulcie said but I'll be long gone by then.'

Barton looked at me sideways.

He held out the brace of fish for me in a manner that was almost aggressive. A taunt of sorts. A challenge. They were close to my face, their lean flanks glistening. They smelled of nothing.

'Here you are, then, lad.'

'The thing is, I'm actually heading off now.'

'Off?' said Barton, slightly affronted. 'Where to?'

I nodded down the coast. 'South.'

'Well, what's so bloody good down there?'

'I don't know. I thought I'd find out.'

The fish were still held close to my face. I looked into the ruined mirrors of their pupils and saw the deep green and magnesium striped pattern of their lean but muscular flanks, their bellies the colour of molten lead. A hint of obscene pink within the gills. Their metallic sheen.

'It'll not take you long,' he said. 'What's an hour or two out of the rest of your life? I'll square up with the old bird later.'

I moved from one foot to the other. Hours were precious and the bay, lovely as it was, appeared to be conspiring to keep me captive.

'It'll not kill you,' said Barton.

'Alright.'

I took the fish from him. He seemed to soften then.

'She's a fine cook, is Dulcie. Some folk down bay call her nutty but she's just her own lady, that's all. Lives the life she wants to lead.'

'Did she never marry?' I asked.

Barton crouched again and locked the straps on his basket. I was still holding the brace aloft.

'You'd have to ask her, and even then she'd only tell you what she wanted to tell you.' He stood again. 'You'd best get them mackerel up there and into the pantry. The day's warming nicely.'

He lifted a basket and hauled it over one shoulder.

'How did you know I was me, Mr Barton?'

He looked away. He squinted out to sea.

'Just did.'

Dulcie did not seem surprised to see me return to her cottage. Her tone, though, I noted, was curt. 'Your hair is wet. Why?'

'I've had a dip.'

'In the sea?'

'Yes. It was freezing.'

'Of course it was. It's the sea. It's a terrible risk.'

'I was quite safe.'

'No one is safe in the sea. It's prone to cruelty, trust me. And you've brought me those, have you?'

'Mr Barton asked me to deliver them to you.'

'All the way from down there?'

'Yes.'

'What did his last slave die of?'

I shrugged.

'And what about your voyage south?'

'Well, he was quite insistent.'

'I'll not eat all these myself, even with Butler's help. So you'll have to stay for tea, I suppose.'

'Oh, no,' I said, even though I was once again famished after the swim and the hike up the hill.

'Well, alright. The fish were a gift for both of us, though. Barton only usually fetches up half what he's given us today.'

I looked down to the bay, to the sea, and to Ravenscar beyond.

'I'll stuff them with fresh fennel and spinach,' said Dulcie.

'I don't want to impose.'

'So don't, then.'

'What's fennel?' I asked.

'Right. You're staying. Butler will be delighted.'

I was back again.

———

It was evening when we ate, though this time I refused wine.

'Did you find somewhere to kip tonight?' Dulcie asked.

'Not yet.'

'Take the shack again if you like. It's grubby but I imagine it's better than bivvying out under canvas.'

Butler sat beside Dulcie, her hand placed on his head. I picked up a final flake of fish from my plate.

'May I?'

'Of course.'

I held it out and the dog snatched it, and then greedily licked at my fingers.

'What was it used for originally? The shack, I mean.'

Dulcie fed some bread to the dog.

'It was a studio,' she said.

'An artist's studio?'

'Yes. Was. Still is, I suppose.'

'It's a great location for one. Are you an artist?'

'Oh, no. Not me.'

'A writer?'

'No, I have not been stricken with that curse either, thank Christ.'

'But you tell such good stories, Dulcie.'

'Telling isn't selling.'

'It looks like it could do with patching up,' I said. 'A lick of paint.'

'I've no call for it.'

'I saw there's a log burner in there too.'

'I had it put in for the colder months.'

'Did you build it?'

'Yes. Well, no. Not with my own hands. I helped design it.'

For a few moments the only sound was the dog chewing his bread. I was suddenly aware of the silence and stillness of Dulcie's overgrown corner, and not just how tranquil it was, but how isolated it might be too. Only then did I feel the faintest glimmer of the loneliness, cold like a shard of ice, that she perhaps experienced deep down inside. Before I knew it I was blurting out a suggestion.

'I could fix it up for you if you like.'

'Whatever for?'

'I just thought it needs protecting before the damp gets into it entirely.'

'Let the damp have it. The cottage is enough for me.'

'A lick of paint and a clear-out is all it needs. It'll help preserve it. Give it a new lease of life before the meadow swallows it up entirely.'

'The meadow is welcome. It hardly seems worth it.'

'Even so. It's still a good cabin.'

'Well, look, Robert, if you want to waste your time on it I won't object. I have little to no use for the studio now but I will insist on reimbursing you.'

'I don't need paying. It'll only take a day. Two at the most. One to clean it out and undercoat it, a second for another layer.'

'You'll still need feeding, though. I insist. There's plenty of paint in the lean-to. Use that. Brushes too, though Christ knows what state they're in. Use what you can find.'

'And then when it's done – '

'You'll be on your way?'

'Yes.'

'Then it looks like we have a deal.'

Bemused, Dulcie's crooked smile turned into a full beam as she raised her glass and we clinked drinks, hers half-full of wine and mine with cool spring water that had a faint hue of the earth to it.

'Very good,' she said. 'Very good.'

The light was fading rapidly and my forearms still itching with inflammation when Dulcie picked up a very small snail shell, long since vacated by its inhabitant. She held it up and examined it closely.

'See this? That's a Fibonacci pattern. It's nature's numbering system, where certain plants and insects and animals follow what is known as the golden ratio. Humans too. Studies have been made. In a world of chaos, I find it gratifying to know we can still find order.'

'I don't quite understand.'

'Well, it really is one of the most amazing natural things. It's all about proportion, you see. I'm afraid I don't know the technicalities but it's something to do with each number being the sum of the previous two numbers. It's an increasing sequence, first detected in the breeding of rabbits. It's there in pine cones and pineapples. The positioning of leaves on a stem. They say it can be found running through the middle of bananas and apples – we can check that later if you like. It's there in seashells and artichokes and ferns and the spiralling carapace of this beautiful peripatetic gastropod's home – a more beautifully engineered creature you will not find. The Fibonacci pattern. The Fibonacci sequence. It's one of life's many mysterious mathematical wonders.'

'I wasn't taught anything so interesting as this at school,' I said, and it was true, for already my schooling was fading into a blur of boring teachers entirely lacking the verve and enthusiasm shown by Dulcie when in full flow on certain chosen subjects. If one or two had been only half as engaging I might have been inclined to stay on. Still, I must have looked rather baffled as she continued.

'The natural world is full of them. Look, I'll show you another. Take off your boot, will you.'

'My boot?'

'Yes, please.'

I did as she asked and unlaced my boot.

'Now. Take your hand and stretch it out – that's it, full stretch. Right, so from the tip of your thumb to the tip of your little finger is your handspan. Now, place it over your face. A bit lower now, Robert.'

I placed my palm on my nose and held it there. I found the span of my hand fit my face almost exactly.

'Now,' she said, 'a perfect fit, from thumb to littlest fingertip.'

I lowered my hand.

'But why did I have to remove my boot?'

'Oh, yes. Now try the same handspan measurement on your foot.'

I did and found that too fit.

'And now your forearm,' said Dulcie.

The same result.

'You can place your foot on your forearm and you'll see that that fits too, though we know that already. And now the final thing you need to do is sniff the boot.'

'Sniff my boot?'

'That's right. Stick your nose in and take a big hit.'

I brought the boot up and inhaled its stale leather interior, smelling the sweat of many a summer mile. I pulled a face.

'And what are your findings?'

'It pongs a bit.'

'Exactly.'

'But what does that have to do with the Fibonacci pattern, Dulcie?'

'Precisely nothing. This is my polite way of saying that your feet hum, Robert, and if we are to continue our little chats in future you might want to consider giving your boots an airing and perhaps a dash of talcum from time to time.'

I rose at first light and walked to a pool in the stream that was deep enough for me to sit in up to my waist. I scrubbed myself with a clump of moss, taking extra care to clean between my toes, and then washed my spare pair of socks.

There was no sign of Dulcie when I began to clear out the shack, moving first the pieces of furniture stacked in

the corner out into the meadow and then the empty bottles, lampshades and broken picture frames. Next followed
two ashtrays, the wadded rags and a palette of paints, each
coloured cube cracked and arid like desert earth. There
was a cardboard box containing various newspapers from
the early 1930s plus a string-tied stack of photographs,
theatre programmes and other printed items. I began to
thumb through them and saw ticket stubs, party invita-
tions, scribbled pages torn from notepads and many lists
containing the names of people and places, errands and
items, but as I rifled through I felt a pang of voyeuristic
guilt. Here were lives into which I had not been entirely
invited. I continued for a curious lingering moment
longer, then stopped and hurriedly replaced them.

Beside the stack was a small brown suitcase, its locks
turned turquoise with decay. I prised them open. Inside
was a file containing a typed manuscript also tied, but
this time with the pink ribbon commonly used for legal
documents. It was thin in my hand.

Placed on top of the manuscript was a curious item
that I lifted out. It was made from a number of drab rags
that had a washed-out appearance, each tied to a circle
made from a wooden rod – hazel, perhaps – and bound
and tightly lagged with further strips of cloth. A string
was attached to the circular frame so that it might be
suspended. In amongst the ragged strands was a handmade rosette and dangling through the centre of it was
a pair of white elbow-length gloves, the palms clasped
together by a single stitch as if in prayer. When I lifted

it up to its full length, the strips dangled the way the bladderwrack seaweed that I had seen the previous day reaches up from the rocks that it clings to, but in reverse.

The item was strange and inexplicable and it unnerved me, so I gently laid it aside and as I did the morning sun beamed into the studio, dazzling me for a moment; I turned my back to it and untied the knotted pink string of the manuscript.

On the front in typed letters it said:

The Offing
by
Romy Landau

Curious, I held it for a moment then replaced it.

An hour or so later I walked back down to the bay and bought from an ironmonger's some fresh paintbrushes, white spirit, varnish, sandpaper, nails and various other things that I required.

The shopkeeper's eyes followed me around the store but when I presented the money Dulcie had given me to pay her monthly bill, her face brightened and she tallied up my items.

'You're the lad from the north country I heard about,' she said.

'Yes. I expect so.'

'A relative of Dulcie's, are you?'

'No.'

Feeling slightly protective, I did not care to elaborate until I knew the purpose of this woman's questioning. Village life might have shown me the destructive power of idle corner-shop gossip, but it had also taught me the art of discretion.

She looked at my supplies. 'A handyman, then?'

'I suppose so, in a way.'

'A bit of company will be nice for her. It must be lonely up on that hillside, after everything she's been through.'

'She has her dog.'

She shook her head. 'Scant consolation. Terrible. Terrible business.'

'Yes,' I said, before asking, 'What was it that happened, exactly?'

'That's Miss Piper's business,' she said, passing me the bag. 'It's hers and hers alone; she'll no doubt let you know if or when you need to know. It's certainly not my place to start flapping my tongue to every passing tradesman.'

I could tell that the shopkeeper wanted to say more – or at least wanted me to enquire further so that she could take some small sadistic pleasure in refusing me again, and the way she said 'tradesman' was weighted with condescension – but instead I thanked her, then turned and left to slowly walk home. Though I was curious, I had no desire to be drawn into the complex web woven by people like the shopkeeper. Instead I bought some crab sticks and slowly chewed them as I climbed the steep track out of the village. They were like pieces of rubber inner tube that had been dredged from the ocean floor.

I took a longer, looping route back via a small church that I had seen far across the fields from Dulcie's hollow. It sat at the crossroads of three back roads, and as I approached it I saw that its cemetery, a walled-off, steep, sloping triangular patch of hillside containing closely stacked headstones, was inhabited by a dozen rare-breed sheep, their shorn coats as dark as coke dust and their yellow eyes indifferent to my presence. They raised their heads in unison for a moment, and then collectively continued to chew at the grass that was growing around the burial plots as I climbed a stile to walk amongst the graves.

They were quite unlike any I had seen. Several stones were carved to represent different aspects of nautical life – knotted ropes, anchors and leaping fish all featured – and the epitaphs told of lives lost to storms. Several of them, I noted, were mariners drowned on the same day. Others featured engravings of agricultural implements such as scythes, forks, rakes and winnowing flails. One or two were mounted with stone engravings of hands clasped in friendship, and many featured the same few family names.

The plots were well tended by the sheep as they trimmed their way around the final resting places of men with old biblical names such as Obadiah, Ezekiel and Aloysius who had died a century or so earlier. They were positioned so that the weathered slabs of North

Yorkshire stone faced out to the sea that had taken many of these lives, and were in fact mere memorial markers for bodies never found.

The church itself was a small box of sandstone with a tiny bell tower no taller than a chimney stack. In the top corner of the portico was built a swallow's nest of mud and grass, from which there came the insistent call of chicks, and when I climbed up onto the bench to gain a better look I was met by four upturned heads with their beaks awaiting worms and open so wide I could see the thin pink membranes of their throats.

I pushed at the grainy oak door and stepped into the church's shadowed interior.

It was cool and still and perfumed with the scent of centuries: dust, polish, old worn cushions, leather, wet coats, candlewax and oil all combined to evoke a tingle of fear that one experiences when faced with the awesome architectural spectacle of faith manifest.

I passed a table laid with dead flowers, a visitors' book and a donation box, and walked down the central aisle, which, like the badger-inhabited lanes that had first delivered me here, was a sunken declivity worn away by the shuffling feet of generations of believers. The church was narrow but the bowed ceiling was like an upturned schooner, much higher than it appeared from the outside. My boots echoed up to the old curved beams overhead.

Each row of pews was entered through a door at chest height, so that anyone sitting in there would have to tilt their head up towards the pulpit, behind which light shone through a simple stained-glass window to illuminate a large crucifix whose shadow stretched for five times its actual length. Proportions were distorted and angles appeared altered, as if I were in the world's most austere seaside-fairground funhouse.

Wooden steps led up to some stalls on a steep and narrow balcony that watched over the nave, and as I climbed them each step creaked uneasily. Only then did I see I was not alone, for at the back of the church, hunched over at the far end of the penultimate row, was a woman, her head bowed and her shoulders silently shaking.

If she had seen me enter – and she can hardly have failed to – she did not acknowledge me, and I suddenly felt like an intruder upon her grief. An agnostic imposter.

I turned to leave and as I did I saw hanging from the ceiling several of the very same curious mobile-like creations that I had found in the suitcase in the shack. These ones appeared to be made from older cloth trimmings and hung suspended on twine from ceiling beams like jellyfish in the deepest offshore waters.

As I passed the woman I saw that she was not old and had in her lap the folded cap of a soldier. Overcome with loss, she did not look up as I lifted the latch on the door and carefully closed it behind me.

VII

That night in the shack I was stirred awake again by a truffling sound close by. Very slowly I sat upright and peered over the windowsill to see a badger not more than ten feet away, rooting at the soft soil. It was large and grey and had its back turned to me, stooped in such a way that I thought of the war widow I had seen weeping in the stillness of the evening, and again I felt a guilty sense of voyeurism, but immense luck too at being privy to this moonlit moment of solitude.

The big old badger's coat was coarse, and the creature so close I could gain a measure of its long claws as it scraped at the soil amongst the first unfurling fronds of early summer bracken, and its sharp, slightly yellowed incisors as it gnawed on a long worm as if it were a child chewing on a cherry bootlace plucked from a penny poke of pick-and-mix. Only its face had the familiar black-and-white striped markings.

It slowly ambled away, nose to the ground, oblivious to my rapt presence.

The encounter left me exhilarated, wide awake, sleep now an impossibility, so I lit the lamp and lifted the manuscript that I had found from the briefcase again.

I turned the title page and read the table of contents. On the next page its dedication read:

For Dulcie
Spinner of honey

I read a poem entitled 'Exeunt (or *White Horses*)' and when I finished it I read it again. Though I felt like a trespasser of sorts and there were words and images in it that I did not understand – nor was I certain of its specific meaning or message, if indeed it had anything so tangible – the poem awoke unfamiliar sensations within me. In that moment new feelings of confusion and curiosity unfolded, more than anything it was an overwhelmingly powerful awareness of sense of place, this place in the here and now, as if the words had crept across the paper and fallen off the page to gather all around me like vines that pulled me back into the poem, so that the imagined lines and the real world somehow merged into a deeper portrait of the land and sea. I read it a third time.

The next poem was called 'Unmothering'. I read that too. I read them all, and then when I finished I went back to the beginning and read them all again.

There was still much I did not understand, yet I did not feel daunted by the unfamiliar form of poetry in *The Offing*, nor confused by the complicated language; far from it, in fact. Whoever she was, Romy Landau's lines were clear and brought to life a world I recognised. Here were images that I knew, of places that I had recently experienced, and her choice of words almost alchemical or incantatory in their effect. These were works written right here where I sat, in this very shack, a world alive with sea fog swirling across the meadow and birds' nests and, yes, badgers skulking through the predawn murk. Each read like a message folded into a bottle and cast away on the tide of time directly to me. The poems were freshly sprung from *this* quiet corner of *this* hillside overlooking *this* coastline. I felt the poems, and that was enough.

I returned the papers to the briefcase and lay back down on my sleeping bag as the waking sun painted long fingers of light across the ceiling of the shack, and the meadow steamed with morning dew, and it was as if a switch had been flicked inside me. I was tired but wide awake as the voice of the poet echoed long after I had set the manuscript aside. The feeling was not that of exhilaration but unease. Heavy with images of doom and foreboding, her work was both haunting and haunted and quite unlike the archaic and incomprehensible verses we had been forced to learn by rote in school. Whoever Romy Landau was, her writing felt modern, as if shaped by recent, very real events. The poems were like a series of mirrors turned inwards, forever reflecting themselves into nothingness. Death stalked the pages, of that I was certain. Each poem raised questions.

I lay there pondering *The Offing* as all of the colours of the summer's morning appeared to flood the room at once.

———

I worked on the shack all the next day. It soon became apparent that if it was to be wrestled back from the encroaching meadow, from the damp and the creepers and the mould and the rodents, then there were a number of small tasks that needed doing.

First of all I set about removing the front door and then reattaching it so that it was airtight. I did this by shaving, sanding and varnishing the frame, and then installing a new set of hinges; it was a two-man job and therefore took twice as long as it should have, and there was much huffing and puffing, and one jammed fingernail beneath which a blood blister quickly blossomed. I then replaced a window latch that had come loose, cut a square of roofing felt to replace a section in the corner that had perished, and then adjusted the taps in the tiny bathroom, which, aside from a patina of mould that covered part of one wall and minimal adjustments to the cistern, was otherwise fine.

Late in the morning Butler heralded Dulcie's arrival with a single bark as she pushed through the long grass. She was carrying a tray of sandwiches.

'I'll leave these here for you.'

'Thank you,' I said. 'Do you want to see what I've done?'

'Not especially. I trust your judgement, Robert.'

She seemed reluctant to enter the shack, whose contents were scattered about in the grass. She cast her eyes across them now.

'I can smell a fox.'

'A fox?'

'Yes,' said Dulcie. 'The acrid funk of a vulpine interloper. Can't you?'

'I'm afraid my head is full of varnish fumes.'

'Look – Butler has picked it up too.'

I turned and watched as the dog sniffed the ground behind the shack, his nose hovering an inch above it like a metal detector being waved across the surface of a ploughed field. He stopped and cocked a leg.

'I doubt you'll see old Reynard,' said Dulcie before I could tell her about the badger's early morning visitation. 'Not with Butler dribbling piss everywhere.'

'Who's Reynard?'

'The fox, of course.'

'Do they all have names?'

'All foxes are Reynard.'

'But why?'

'Well, the fox plays a significant role in our indigenous folklore, though – believe it or not – his moniker is German in origin. As I recall, it comes from Reinhard, or some such derivative. An anthropomorphised fox-man figure has seemingly stalked European mythology since time immemorial. He's there in Chaucer, haunting the dreams of a talking cockerel. He's a trickster, a villain to many but an anti-hero full of merciless guile to others.'

'The farmers kill them round our way.'

'I shouldn't wonder, the brutes. An act of true barbarism.'

'But they kill the chickens.'

Dulcie sighed. 'And so do humans. But should we be hunted, trapped, maimed, poisoned, ensnared, shot or torn to pieces by a pack of idiot beagles?'

I smiled. 'I could think of one or two people who I'd do that to.'

Dulcie laughed and offered me a sandwich. I took one. 'Such as?'

'There was one boy at school. Dennis Snaith.'

'I dislike him already,' said Dulcie. 'For that is the name of a snitch or a bully, I'd wager.'

'Both,' I said.

'And what did this worthless slug-boy do to incur your wrath?'

'He broke my nose in a game of British Bulldog.'

'The rotten runny shit.'

'Yes. I thumped him for it, though.'

'Good for you. Good for you. Sometimes you have to speak the only language these people understand.'

I bit into my sandwich and chewed a mouthful of egg and cress. Dulcie reached into her pocket.

'I have salt.'

'Oh, no, thank you.'

She reached into another. 'Pepper?'

'It's great as it is.'

'Well, I'll leave you to it.'

'But I haven't shown you what else needs doing, and what I found.'

'Found?'

'Yes. There was some rubbish that I thought perhaps could be thrown out – empty bottles and the like.'

'Get rid of it. Get rid of it all.'

'But there was also this.'

Dulcie followed me into the shack. I wiped my hands on my trousers and reached for the suitcase, then pulled out the manuscript of poems.

'I don't have my spectacles, I'm afraid,' said Dulcie. 'And I have a million things to do.'

She turned away.

'It's a collection of poems,' I said. 'Dedicated to you. It's called – '

'*The Offing.*'

Dulcie looked at me for a moment, and I saw for the first time something in her face I had not yet seen – a quiet despair, perhaps. Something desperate contained behind a rigid facade. A pained reluctance.

'I know,' she said, her voice strained. 'And you've read some of it?'

'A little,' I lied. 'I hope you don't mind.'

'Why would I? It's not my work.'

'Still.'

'Poems belong to the world. One chooses to read or not. They are bigger than any one person.'

'Would you like to see them?' I held the manuscript out.

'See them?'

'Yes.'

'Robert, I practically lived them. I don't need to read them.'

'There was also this.' I held up the item made from rags. 'I wondered what it was.'

Dulcie did not take it. Instead she half-turned towards the meadows. Towards the sea.

'If you really must know, it's called a maiden's garland.'

'I saw one very similar in the church along the lane.'

'You went to the church?'

'Yes.'

'It's symbolic.'

'What does it symbolise?'

There was a long pause.

'Purity.'

When I didn't respond, Dulcie said: 'Sexual purity. They're made for funerals.'

'In the church they were hanging from the ceiling like decorations.'

She sighed. 'As I said, it is symbolic. They're placed on the heads of those who are purported to have died chaste.'

'Chaste?'

'Pure. Allegedly. Virginal. They are for those who have died before their time. Hamlet's poor Ophelia wore one when she was found in her watery grave, put there by her own volition.'

She frowned, took a breath and then continued.

'Yes, in days gone by, death by one's own hand meant a burial in non-consecrated ground; no Christian church-yard would accept them, which is nothing less than callous in my book, but of little surprise. To his credit, Shakespeare at least had his king bend the rules a little: "Yet here she is allowed her virgin crants / Her maiden strewments, and the bringing home / Of bell and burial." "Crants" is another word for the garland. So her "peace-parted soul" departed with such an item atop her flowing fiery locks.'

A silence fell upon on us and I was suddenly aware that the shack was a room built for one. Its dimensions encouraged a physical closeness that in this moment felt awkward as that silence sat there, a vacant space waiting to be filled.

'Why do you have one, Dulcie?'

'Because I do.'

I hesitated.

'Is it anything to do with these poems?'

'You ask too many questions.'

'I'm sorry.'

'And still you apologise too much.'

I hesitated.

'I'm not sorry about that.'

'That's the correct response. You're nearly forgiven.'

She held her hand out. I passed her the file and the maiden's garland.

'Everything,' she said. 'One has everything to do with the other.'

She opened the file and glanced at the first page and then flapped it shut again. She turned away and looked back into the middle distance. I noticed then that her eyes were wet, and her face wore a look of ever-greater desperate concern.

'Not once have I cried in front of anyone.'

She turned away, shielding her face.

'Not once, even at the funeral, did I come close. Even then. Until now, that is.'

Butler appeared then and circled us, a look of curiosity on his face.

'I'm sorry if I upset you.'

'I told you to stop apologising.'

The file dangled in her hand as she turned back to me.

'Well, I suppose now is as good or as bad a time as any.'

'For what?'

'For me to explain everything.'

I tried to speak. I tried to say something honest and wise and compassionate, but perhaps I was too young to fully possess any of these attributes. Instead my face reddened and I felt a little nauseous, and wished that the dog would choose this moment to make a demand. I was capable of uttering nothing but broken sentences.

'You don't have to – ' I paused and then tried again. 'What I mean is – '

'Too late,' said Dulcie. 'The floodgates are creaking under the strain. One thing, though.'

'Yes.'

'We're going to need a gallon of tea and I believe it's your turn. Finish your sandwiches first, though. Then come up to the house.'

'Her name meant "obstinate" or "rebellious". Romy. We met in London. She was a poet fast becoming brilliant, even then. Not in her writing – she was still an undergraduate finding her way – but the manner in which she lived her life: unrestrained and not at all in possession of the vinegary disposition of German stereotyping. You see, Robert, her existence itself was poetic: her clothes, her humour, her laughter. The way she held herself. And, let me tell you, the pursuit of bohemian individualism in 1933 was not encouraged – ironic, given the geographical origins of the term.'

We were in Dulcie's living room – what she called the parlour. I was sitting in an armchair, but she preferred to stand. Twice she nearly banged her head on a small chandelier whose decorative pieces of glass cast patterns upon faded wallpaper that showed interwoven willow leaves on a beige background.

'Anyway. So. The writing was on the wall, written in bold yellow stars. A person of her nature couldn't be expected to stay in a country ruled by thugs and propped up by acolytes, so as soon as the Führer's arse bones were firmly planted on the top pot Romy packed her bags. Wrote her way out, actually. A scholarship. She could have gone to Oxbridge but claimed that she couldn't find it on the map so plumped for our fair capital instead. Which is where I met her. She was a magnet for many but none felt the pull stronger than me.'

'You and her – '

' – were quite impervious to a significant age difference, not to mention the judgement of others? Is that what you were going to say? In which case, affirmative, but please, no other questions, Robert. I'll tell you what I tell you.'

Dulcie continued.

'So yes, just to further evoke the ire of the critics and the bores and bigots, she was a great deal younger than me, but then Romy was a great deal of everything to everyone, all of the time. Faster, funnier, gayer and with a rapier wit perfect for bursting the fat old-money fools that fell at her feet. She just had to find a way to express herself and with some gentle steering from yours untruly that outlet, it transpired, was poetry. By the time she graduated – a high second, she sobbed with disappointment for a week – I was tiring of London and the same dismal faces, the dreary get-to-gethers, the tittle-tattle and the fuss of it, the endless parade of lords and viscounts, ignoble scions and silly little minor royals, and it was clear she was in desperate need of total relaxation because, Robert, what you have to understand is that Romy's mind ran at two hundred miles an hour all the time, and the both of us enjoyed more than a drink or two, but whereas I found a couple of aspirin, a raw egg and a big sleep would see me right as rain after we had tied one on, she would have these most awful mental and physical collapses where she would not be able to leave her room for days. Then she was a spent husk, an empty shell. Just an awful mess. It went beyond the boozing, and into something far deeper and darker. My father had kept this place as a bolt-hole for aeons, for his illicit weekend rendezvous I shouldn't wonder, so we began to spend time here, in order for Romy to rest and write while I could garden and cook and paint and breathe and think, and the two of us could just *be*. Together. Here in the perfect refuge. We swapped gossip and gin and smoggy coughing fits for clean air, fresh food and, in Romy's case, daily swims out there. She had a steeliness to her and took to it like – well, just like you. Claimed it helped refresh her mind, and certainly it seemed to work wonders. In these moments she looked lit up.'

I nodded. Dulcie seemed to be searching her memory for the correct words.

I took a drink from my cup and then set it down. She continued.

'And so she wrote the bulk of her first collection in this house, which I edited, and of course it went on to be a huge success that no one but I had envisaged because if I have a talent for one thing, Robert, it is seeing dormant potential, and then awakening it. Some create, others facilitate. I am the latter. A cajoler. A prodder. The perfect patron. Anyway, the critics were soon hailing a unique new voice in European poetry and Eliot wrote and young Wystan Auden wrote and Will Yeats said some lovely things and Robert Frost sent a telegram from over the water – Pound was sniffy but that was no surprise – and then that was that. Romy had arrived, and her life took on a new dimension. We travelled. We travelled to so many places. We saw the souks of Marrakesh. The temples of Tulum. The ruins of Pompeii. America, of course, which was marvellously gluttonous and vulgar, and suited us just fine. We even went to Iceland. And of course we visited most of the major European cities, where she gave readings and charmed the press everywhere she went. Romy was very much in demand, and once again the carousel of life spun faster still. Gin for breakfast, champagne for luncheon and a trail of unpaid room-service bills, all of that. Europe was so beautiful then.'

She paused for a moment and then spoke in a faraway voice.

'Perhaps it will be again soon.'

Dulcie crossed the room and lifted a small framed picture from the wall. She passed it to me.

It held within it a photograph of a young woman who was more beautiful than I had imagined. Her chin was tilted slightly upwards in a pose that made her look as if she was silently challenging the photographer somehow, and her skin was so clean and clear it appeared to glow. Her lips were unpainted and slightly parted to show her teeth, which were crooked in a way that I found exciting, and even though the picture was monochromatic I could see that she had brilliant blue eyes that were at odds with the colour of her hair, which was worn quite short and as black as Whitby jet. I immediately wanted to look at more pictures of her, to see her from other angles. To know more.

'She looks very nice,' I said, too embarrassed to express my truly feelings. 'Like – '

'Like?'

'Like someone famous. A film star.'

Dulcie took the picture from me and stole only the briefest of glances at it.

'What was her book called?' I asked.

'*The Emerald Chandelier,*' Dulcie said, returning the frame to the wall. 'So back and forth we went, from sea to city, for engagements and readings and dinners where Romy was often the guest of honour because there's nothing literature likes more than hailing a new darling – "fresh meat" might be a better way of putting it – and for a brief and brilliant moment she was it. There was something almost protean in the way she adapted to the various roles expected of her: commentator, comic, wit, visionary. But all the while things were deteriorating back at home.'

'In London?'

'No. In the motherland. Or rather the Fatherland. Germany, where her work was not in print. Nationalism was approaching fever pitch, the nescient pro-war bores were winning and those who were published faced one of two equally grim choices: either submit to censorship from those illiterate beasts who were in charge, or go into exile. Romy had already chosen the latter, though I know she dreamed always of one day returning. It wasn't that life here with me, and with her writing success, was just not quite enough, but rather that she had a point to prove. The Führer and his types were the opposite of everything she – everything *we* – stood for, and to never return would be to submit entirely. To give up. Plus, of course, her family was there.'

'Fighting the Nazis?'

'Well, no. Not necessarily. Let's just say that an ideology that monumental does not gain power without the complicity of a sizeable portion of the population, and leave it at that.'

'So some of her family were on the other side.'

'Of course, of course. Nationalism is an infection, Robert, a parasite, and after years of recession many were willing hosts. The tide had too rapidly turned against all things Germanic here also. The prevailing question was: what does one do when rejected at home, yet hailed as a sage abroad – even if only fleetingly – but then just as swiftly renounced again purely because of the soil on which one happens to have been born? Romy had barely drawn breath before she found herself rejected on both sides: by the grubby scrum of English critics who had praised her, but who now had to be seen to be questioning every single comma lest they be accused of being unpatriotic, and by those over the water in her homeland, where Romy's voice had simply not been given an outlet. Her readers retreated, the publishers fell silent and all those sycophantic contemporaries who had scrabbled to laud her work mysteriously stopped writing. Her creative fire, once raging so ferociously, had been dampened by national-istic fervour and ignorant *twots*. She was stymied.'

'Well, I don't know anything about poetry but I enjoyed the poems that I read,' I said. 'She sounds like a very talented person.'

'She was,' said Dulcie. 'She was. Very special.'

She fell silent. In my naivety it was only then in that awkward, still moment that I realised that perhaps the maiden's garland had belonged to Romy, or been used to mark her passing. But I did not dare mention it because, as Dulcie had said, she would tell me what she would tell me. Her tears were not for a broken relation-ship but a lost life. A tragedy unspoken.

'As you can well see, the cottage is poky, and seems to shrink during these bloody endless winters that blow in from the Baltic, and of course back then it was still full of the gimcrack trinkets of my father's many mistresses, so we had Romy installed in the meadow. Domiciled in the Yorkshire wild. I had the studio especially built for her. A bespoke commission. It was a place in which she would write, with a beautiful view of the meadow and down to the bay. A desk, a wood burner. Even a little cot bed. Everything she needed. *The Emerald*

Chandelier was a metaphor, you see. For the breaking waves, and the way they fling green jewels into the sunlight, and the infinity of it all. From here she would plot her comeback. Her renaissance, if you will.'

'I can see that it must have been a nice place to work before it became overgrown.'

Dulcie's face had darkened again.

'Perhaps it was,' she said quietly. 'Perhaps. But impending war is difficult to ignore, and loss of one's nerve even more so.'

She took another drink of tea and then looked around.

'Where is that dog?' She stood up and called his name, and the dog came through from the kitchen. 'Oh, there you are.'

Butler stood there for a moment and then, seeing that his services were not required, he turned and left again.

'I expect you want to know what happens next.'

'You don't have to tell me. Really, you don't.'

Dulcie sighed. All the while she had been standing but now she finally sat down, as if exhausted from the sharing of her story. She flopped heavily into an armchair and reached for a folded newspaper, which she wafted in front of her face like a fan. But she could only sit still for a moment, because then she pulled herself to her feet again and became busy around the room doing not much at all.

'The war happened next,' she said with her back turned to me. 'And a lot more besides. We should have more tea. Do you want tea? Or maybe something stronger?'

I shook my head. 'I'm fine, thanks.'

'I'll make some anyway.'

As Dulcie squeezed past me into the kitchen to fill a kettle and set it on the stove, then returned to fetch the teapot, caddy and strainer, which she kept in a large cabinet alongside a mismatched selection of cups, plates and cutlery that seemed to have been collated from a wide variety of sets, I was aware of how small the cottage was, and indeed how it could be seen to shrink during the long dark days of winter. It was enough for two compatible people, so long as they were in good spirits.

'Do you think there will be another world war?' I asked.

Listless, she paused in the doorway, swaying slightly. Her hands were full and her reply was emphatic. 'Oh, yes.'

'A third one? You really think so?'

'With great certainty. I'd bet my house, my hat and my horse on it.'

'Do you have a horse?'

'No, but I did – several. To call it a third war is misleading, though.'

'But how can you be sure?'

'Because there is always a war being waged some-where, and we never learn a damn thing from any of them. Mankind exists in conflict, and always will so long as it is called "mankind". Nothing changes. And anyway, a third war will probably be a final war.'

'Don't you believe in progress, though, Dulcie?'

She came through from the kitchen, placed the tray bearing empty cups on the side and then flopped down into the chair for a second time.

'Not in a linear way, no. I don't think we are continually improving, if that's what you mean. We may learn lessons, but we don't apply them. It's always one step forward, two steps back. Then a leap sideways. Then diagonally. Do you see what I mean?'

I must have twisted my face in confusion, as Dulcie elaborated.

'Take your cathedral again. A magnificent building. Celestial. Constructed to evoke awe and wonder amongst all who chanced upon it – and nearly a thousand years old. A miracle of the imagination, as if God himself had drawn up the blueprint.'

'I thought you didn't believe in – '

'Shush, I'm making a broader point. Now. Pan out from the picture and what do you see – a city, yes, fine. What else? I'll tell you what: drab municipal buildings built from cheap concrete, uniform mass-produced bricks and – oh, my eyes – the epitome of bad taste, pebble-dash. Not just your city, but almost every town or city. I'm talking about civic buildings as easy on the eyes as an astigmatism; buildings built to evoke feelings of – what? Nothing but ennui and lassitude. A sinking feeling. A cruelty played by planners with no spark whatsoever. If they had their way the entire country would be pebble-dashed, metaphorically speaking.'

Dulcie was really warming up now.

'Who are they?' I asked.

'Oh, you know. *Them*. The janitors of mediocrity. The custodians of drab and peddlers of dreck. Men, mainly. Where once we built towers to heaven, now we build frumpy sweatboxes for pen-pushers. After nine hundred years I don't call that progress. Not a jot. We're moving backwards, forwards and sideways all at once. We're oscillating, Robert. We live in chaos and out of chaos comes war. I could put it a more simple way for you, if you like: the Great War was the worst atrocity committed by humankind. What lessons were learned? Build bigger bombs and better bombs, that's all. Hitler still happened, and there'll be another angry little man along in due course. I sometimes think that in many ways we're completely screwed, all the time. I suppose it's a collective state of insanity. It must be, to keep repeating the same patterns of death and violence. Romy saw this. Romy knew. She had the poet's insight, you see. Because the true poet looks beyond the lamina of lies, peers into the space between the dimensions. And now I am rather tired. Perhaps a nap.'

'Of course.'

'Perhaps you might like to take Butler for a wander later, after you've finished whatever it is you're doing.'

'I'd be glad to.'

In the kitchen the kettle was whistling like the wind.

The conversation did not continue that night. Perhaps Dulcie had run out of words for now.

After I had taken Butler up onto the moors for a two-hour walk that left my lungs burning and during which I saw my first-ever snake – a fat adder basking in the middle of a narrow old packhorse track that ran through the heather – I returned exhausted.

There was no sign of Dulcie and her curtains were drawn, so feeling rather furtive I boiled four eggs in a pan of water, to which I added a clump of nettle leaves and a twist of lemon. I carried it to the steps of the cabin and carefully peeled each egg, and slowly ate them one by one, and then when the tea had mashed I drank it straight from the pan as the sun slowly set. Then, when the meadow was still and fading from view, I lit a lamp and took out the manuscript that Dulcie had insisted I return to its briefcase in the studio.

Something compelled me to read the poems again. I think it was the desperate look I saw in Dulcie's eyes, and her words that had gone unspoken. An attempt, perhaps, to better understand this strange and brilliant individual that she had described. All the answers as to who she was, and the truth of her friend Romy's life, were to be found in this stack of papers that had, for several years, been touched only by spiders.

This time I paid closer attention to the language, and on a scrap of paper I wrote down all the words that I did not understand alongside those from other poems I had devoured since arriving at Dulcie's. The list read:

islomanes
cumulus
phosphorescent

codicil
meniscus
vellum

hara-kiri
arbutus
whitecaps

shibboleth
anoxia
hypoxia

Saksamaa
Elbe

seppuku

———

Many of the poems remained a mystery during those early nocturnal readings, but enough of a mystery for me to want to unravel their meaning. Sitting there, the oil lamp's flame casting writhing shadows across the pale pages, I felt as if their author was in the cabin with me. That they were conceived in this very place was thrilling, and for the first time I understood what it meant to be haunted, as the more I read, the greater was the sense of loss for the fact that Romy was no longer living, the sense that these poems were in fact messages from the dead, missives sent from a place of abject loneliness. Not only that but they were messages – pleas, even – sent back to their place of creation. Here, where I lay, in a shack, in a meadow in Yorkshire.

It became clear in my untrained, barely read mind that as I progressed through the collection each poem was arranged in such a way that Romy Landau was writing towards her own escape, her own expiration. They were laments for herself, exit spells.

What I had first read as being superficially concerned with a world I instantly recognised – the lanes, the cottage, the meadow and especially the sea – now began to fall away to reveal a complex mind descending into the murk of ultimate and infinite despair. The stark and unflinching horror of the opening lines of one poem in particular, 'Unmothering', struck me like a fencepost rammer.

A womb awaits
      what?
Nothing but a
      child;
a birth-machine you are
      not.

It was the middle of the night when I finished the collection and finally discerned what had happened to Romy. The answer had been there all along, in Dulcie's hatred and mistrust of the sea, and in the maiden's garland. Yet it was only when I read the collection for the third, fourth or fifth time that I, a young man more readily used to wandering the lanes, working with his hands or dreaming what great adventures might lie ahead now the veil of war was lifted, finally understood.

It was one poem in particular that revealed the truth of the matter, the poem that now most commonly features in anthologies, is taught on academic courses and has been read on radio and stage and set to music, and even chiselled into a memorial stone that sits behind a trail that runs deep into the heart of a wood near the Germany–Austria border, but which back then was still just a poem secreted away from the world, and read only by me, the humble son of a hard-working miner:

Exeunt (or *White Horses*)

I leave this land
and give myself to golden water.

How deep, I wonder,
do the sun's tresses

trail, how far the reach of the wretched
figure on the wretched beach,

and what awaits she
who rides white horses

then slips
to swaying darkness

down coralline chains to fingerling roots,
and briny beds

where bestial wails chorus
like carillon chimes

where all is rust and shadow,
and salt-stripped bone.

A snuffed-out sun, the retreating shore.
The perfect undertow seeing her home.

Romy Landau had drowned herself.

VIII

Drizzle fell in the middle of the night and continued through the early hours, slow and persistent, drilling right on through to daybreak, so I stayed inside for most of the morning, first checking the floorboards – I found two had come loose so hammered them back into place and then stained them with varnish to prevent wood-worm – and then working on lengths of skirting that were showing the early signs of rot. I prised out the nails that held them in place and then removed them. Rain thrummed down on the roof once more but then it passed and when I looked out Dulcie's curtains were open, as too was the kitchen window, and the dog was hunched over at the bottom of the meadow, having a quiet moment in the long grass.

Dulcie waved as I approached.

'Fourteen hours,' she said with incredulity. 'I slept for *fourteen hours*. Right through. I can hardly believe it. Have you eaten? Your guts must be growling in protest.'

'I hope you don't mind but I had some eggs last night.'

'With what?'

'Just by themselves. I boiled them.'

'I mind very much that that is all you had, and you're still eating like there's a bloody war on. Good lord, man, you'll be internally impacted for days unless I put some porridge in you. Come in, come in. I've done a pan with a dash of bilberry jam and my own special secret ingredient.'

'What is it?'

'You'll have to guess. It's half the fun.'

Work on the studio continued each day this way for a week, and then two. I patched up the shack and with each small task created a greater problem to be solved. Replacement guttering. A new windowpane. Two new windowpanes. A drain to unblock, a cracked ceramic pipe to unearth and fix.

Stripping, sanding, varnishing.

Patching and painting.

When I wasn't working I was fed increasingly lavish meals by Dulcie, who was an inventive cook working from a rationed diet augmented by ingredients that she managed to source from friends in high places: elaborate meat pies and steamed puddings, home-made pasta, boeuf bourguignon, fruit flans, curries, roast ducks and geese and all manner of other new discoveries. Then, when the tide and the weather allowed, I walked down bay to enjoy a swim most evenings, tumbling and spluttering in the backwash to burn off the calorie-rich food that I was quite unused to.

And each night I slowly read the books that she had given me by lamplight in the creaking shack in the meadow, confused and bored by some, but inspired and energised by others.

Full summer had arrived and I felt my body changing. So lean and pale when I left my home, it was now filling out, seeking a new shape. Cords of narrow muscle ran through my arms and the soft puppy flesh of waist and stomach was hardening from all the stretching and swimming. I felt different too: stronger and more capable. It was a strength that seemed to come from within. All the reaching and chopping and Dulcie's rich home cooking, and the unbroken stretches of sunshine too, had done wonders for my physical form, which had begun to take on a honeyed hue where once it was the colour of proving dough.

I saw the world in a sharper focus too.

And all around my wrists and up my arms were nicks and scratches, scars and stings and welts, each an emblem of outdoor toil, proudly sported like a medal awarded for an unbelievable act of valour.

———

The bay was becoming busier.

I watched as each day the pulsing-hot centre of summer brought people, and the people brought buckets and spades and ham-and-pease-pudding sandwiches wrapped in paper, and boiled eggs and cold ration-book sausages shining greasily with a slick rime of grey fat. They peeled hard-boiled eggs and unscrewed warm bottles of pop, and some had windbreaks or footballs or flimsy little fishing nets fastened to the ends of broom handles, and most had children, and soon they were all turning a parboiled stinging red as they ran amok on the broad beach beneath the relentless sun.

The rock pools became subjects of forensic examination for excitable barefoot boys from the industrial towns of Teesside and West Yorkshire – the locals called them 'diggers' because of their fondness for digging holes – while mothers arranged their packed lunches on blankets, dogs coughed up salt water and irritable fathers slept beneath their handkerchiefs; those who had made it back from the war, anyway. Everyone was glad to be alive, and no one said so.

Just to feel the damp sand between their toes was enough.

And there were girls too. Young women, around my age. So many sullen, cream-coloured women in bathing suits and headscarves, and in bloom, outnumbering the men as they carefully placed their towels apart from parents and younger siblings, whom they disowned with petulant glances of disdain from behind the lenses of their sunglasses.

Each day I saw them, these young ladies, scattered around the beach, some paddling in the shallows in pairs, shrieking at the snapping jaws of the cold North Sea, others reclining to smoke cigarettes alone, with attitude. They occupied that no-man's-land between

adolescence and adulthood, where insecurity and innocence, joy and world-weary cynicism do battle, where
different masks are tried on for size. They seemed utterly
unobtainable to a honking youth from the northern
industrial backcountry such as I.

Some I observed laughing, others pouting, the curved
lines of their legs, hips and arching lower backs as they
skipped and ran and rolled and swam somehow mirror-
ing the sea-carved curves of the cliff that clung to the
coastal reach as it disappeared around corners. They
commandeered the beach for weeks.

I was too stunned by their physical form and considered poise to do much about my infatuations beyond
attempting to offer a shy smile. Even that, to my horror,
was often an impossibility, as the muscles around my
mouth rebelled at the crucial moment and it instead
came out as an awkward twisted grimace smeared across
the blush of my face.

Those that glowered back as I stood towelling myself
dry after an evening swim or, even more wounding,
looked right through me, I found the most beautiful
and beguiling. A withering look from one could crush
the soul and destroy a day, yet the suggestion of a smile
might make me dizzy for hours afterwards.

Frequently I thought about one girl in particular. A
dark-haired young woman, a year or two older than
me, with skin as white as paper. Skin so thin I imagined
that close up it might be possible to see the map of her
inner workings beneath it.

I had only seen her twice, on concurrent days, ankle-deep in the sand at the water's edge, but in my mind I visited her for nights on end, creating increasingly elaborate scenarios that developed from us first engaging in deep and meaningful conversation, to me coming to her aid when she was stung by a jellyfish (though I had seen none) or was stranded on a rocky boulder as the tide came in (I had seen too many matinee screenings of Tyrone Power and Gary Cooper films at the Miners' Institute on Saturdays).

Then, ultimately, it would lead to her, the unnamed young woman, kissing me first on the cheek, and then on the mouth, and then us falling to the sand as the spray washed over us and then –

And then I would feel an ache of longing inside, if only to learn her name.

Perhaps it was Kathleen or Angela or Jeanette or Dorothy. Or maybe something more exotic. Perhaps she was Italian or Spanish or French. Cécile or Carlotta.

Of course, in these fantastical scenarios the beach was devoid of screaming children and small swirls of steaming dog dirt and people munching on pickled eggs, and my mouth was able to smile correctly, and I knew all the right words in all the right order, and everything about me was different, and better.

It was the first time I'd seen women in such a way. Back at home, there were only the schoolgirls of the village, most of whom I had known since birth, or else they were distant cousins or the sisters of schoolmates, all of us shoved together by geography and circumstance, the subsequent overfamiliarity an inevitable consequence of growing up in close proximity. Reinvention was an impossibility too for those who ever sought it, and even minor acts of individual self-expression could bring about ridicule amongst those who claimed some sort of unspoken ownership over your very existence. Veering too far from the place that we were each expected to occupy in the grander scheme of things was rarely rewarded. Quite the opposite. It was assumed that the young were to settle down soon and age quickly, and wear their best suits as their fathers did on a Sunday.

Then there were the older women of the community, some of them strong and heroic, others worn down by worry or cruel and indifferent husbands. Finally there were those few women of the village who were said to leave bottles of HP Sauce in the front window to signal the temporary absence of their husbands to any passing workmen – drivers on the brewery drays, perhaps, or skilled labourers from far-flung towns or villages – though they only appeared to exist in malicious rumour and back-room gossip. If they were in plain sight I might have noticed them, but sex for most of us was a foreign country rarely visited and never discussed. Few females I knew ever frolicked; there was nowhere *to* frolic in a place whose brickwork was dyed black by soot-smoke and whose skies billowed with coke dust and whose surrounding farmed fields of row upon row of ploughed and planted furrows were featureless and functional, nor was there ever much of a reason either. Fewer still would have been at ease showing the world the birthmarks, freckles or moles that decorated their beautiful sun-starved skin as the young ladies did on the beach in the bay that summer.

In time they would leave their various states of repose to return home – to factory jobs, perhaps, or secretarial college; to overbearing fathers, to errant boyfriends or fast-talking fiancés, and then, perhaps, to dreary husbands; to sunless shifts behind desks or on factory floors; to shortening autumn days and long winter nights in dance halls and cafes with steamed-up windows and the stale lingering stink of tobacco smoke, hair oil, decaying English teeth and damp woollen coats. And then, perhaps, in five or ten years' time, there would be babies for some of them, the close confinement of domesticity drawing in, and the slight souring towards all things once thought of as sweet. Worlds shrinking. Some might become their mothers, waking one day to discover with horror that they had married their fathers. Life for most was beyond their control, though I had already made it my singular goal not to fall foul of limited expectation. I hoped many of the young women felt able to do the same.

But for now at least, summer seemed endless and something unfamiliar stirred within me on those evenings as I rolled up my towel and glanced at these free girls of the bay, whose sole purpose appeared to be to stretch and yawn and smile and smoke; to see and be seen.

It was a hunger, perhaps, of a different kind. Something new awakened.

It was desire, and young manhood was undoubtedly within me like a benevolent parasite. It had taken residence and was slowly altering me from the inside, and I was merely a passive host as complex chemicals steered me through the summer. There was little I could do about it. A strange alchemy was underway; there would be no turning back.

———

'Have you written to your mother?' Dulcie called to me one afternoon when I was attempting to sharpen the shears again. They had already become blunted by the stubborn stalks of the thirsty meadow.

With a tinge of guilt I realised that in the several weeks of wandering that had led to here, where the days were now smudging together in one long streak of sunshine broken only by the darkness of falling night at each tired day's end, the thought hadn't crossed my mind, so I said so.

'Well, won't she be worried?' asked Dulcie.

Again, it was not a thought I had entertained. 'I'm sure she's fine. She'll be dead busy.'

'And I'm sure she won't sleep properly until she's at least had a scribbled line from you.'

'Do you think?'

'I know.'

I frowned.

'I have excellent stationery,' said Dulcie. 'You may use it.'

That night, by the light of the lamp, with the dog stretched out beside me on my blankets, I put aside my book, primped up my pillow and sat back to write a note to my mother on stiff paper as grainy and mottled as an eggshell.

Dear Mam,

I hope you and Dad are both keeping well. I am writing to you from a shed in a meadow above a bay in Yorkshire. It is dry and warm, and I am quite well.

The shed belongs to a lady called Dulcie, who I have been doing some odd jobs for. Dulcie is tall. She is taller than any man I have known except perhaps Jack Barclay, though unlike Big Jackie she still has her front teeth and doesn't eat worms.

In fact, she eats a lot yet she is not at all fat. She reminds me of a very long cat and she is not like anyone from the village, or anywhere. Her cooking is second only to yours.

The weather is beautiful here, as I hope it is there. I'd wager the allotment is parched and that Dad's parsnips think their throats have been slit. Are the pigeons flying in this heat? I am turning as brown as a berry, swimming daily and reading lots of books. I am seeing England, or at least a lovely green part of it.

I plan on coming home when the exam results are announced, though I can't quite remember when that is, so if I am not back in time perhaps you might fetch them for me and send them on. I will forward an address if or when I have one.

Warmest wishes,
Robert

P.S. Dulcie has a dog who looks like he is trained to savage all comers but really is very friendly. He is called Butler because he acts like one. He is sitting beside me now. He is the second new friend I have made this summer.

One day, over a very early lunch of sorrel omelettes served with salad and deep-fried beetroot chips, quite out of the blue Dulcie asked, 'Have you read the white horses one, then?'

It took me a moment to realise that she was continuing the conversation that had ended promptly over a fortnight earlier.

'Yes,' I said.

'You're a bright boy.'

I had no reply to this but found myself blushing slightly.

'So you know,' she said.

'Know?'

She fixed me with a slightly stern look.

'You know by now what fate befell her. Or you should if you have half a functioning brain.'

I hesitated before speaking again.

'Did she – '

'Yes?' she interrupted.

'Did she – '

'Go on,' Dulcie said, as if she were intercepting any attempt at a reply.

'Did Romy drown herself?'

Dulcie looked away, out to sea, then back to me.

'Is that what you think happened?'

Again I hesitated, uncertain.

'Yes. I think that's what "White Horses" is about.'

She frowned.

'Then you are correct.'

'I'm sorry. I'm sorry that I'm right, really I am.'

'And what did you think of the poem?'

'It was the saddest thing I've ever read. But – ' The words appeared beyond me, but I reached for them. 'In a strange way, it was beautiful too.'

Dulcie nodded. She nodded for a long time.

'She is in the offing now.'

We finished our omelettes in silence.

'Have you read the collection, Dulcie?' I asked when our plates were clear. 'Have you read *The Offing*? You didn't actually say that you had.'

'Why would I?'

I stammered but Dulcie continued.

'Romy bequeathed it to me.'

'I'm not sure I know what that means.'

'She left it behind, right there in that studio of hers. She put it on the desk in full view and then she walked down the hill and into the sea, and was never seen again. One poem was set aside. "White Horses". A week later I read it, but then I put it all away in an old briefcase and there it has sat ever since. In my grief I was beyond anger. So no, I have not read it. And now you know the truth of it.'

'Did she mean to kill herself?'

Even just saying the words felt awkward, as if I had broken a code of silence. *Kill herself.* When Dulcie did not reply I immediately regretting asking the question, and I wished I were able to retract it. What felt like a long time passed.

'She intended to become immortal,' Dulcie finally said. 'But to do that one must die. And to die like that one must walk away from all that one knows and loves.'

I hesitated, but the need to ask another question felt like a compulsion that I couldn't ignore.

'Why was that poem called "White Horses"?'

'It's more nautical symbolism,' she explained. 'A recurring image, forever scorched upon my retinas. White horses are the breaking waves. The curling crest could be seen as the mane and the crashing surely sounds like hooves thundering across the turf.'

'I didn't understand what "exeunt" means either.'

'Ah, well, that's a theatrical term. Shakespearean. It is used as a direction for leaving the stage. For exiting, usually in the plural, though I think this still works. And now you can put the pieces of the puzzle together.'

I thought it over for a full minute.

'"Exeunt (or *White Horses*)" was Romy's last goodbye before she drowned herself?'

'As I said, you're a bright boy.'

'It's a beautiful way to leave the world,' I said.

'She was a poet. I sometimes think perhaps she was the first pure modernist too. The one who could have opened the door for whatever comes next. A bold new future was within her grasp, I'm sure of it.'

'It's a shame that the world never got to hear her say goodbye.'

Dulcie pursed her lips and looked away. She took a drink of tea.

'And neither did I.'

'Did she leave a note?'

She shook her head. 'Nope. Or if she did it was well hidden. Believe me, I searched the pockets of her clothes, rifled through her possessions. No stone was left unturned. She left nothing but the poems and a Romy-shaped hole in the lives of many. I can tell you, Robert, the silence that followed has been awful. No one should ever have to go through that sense of suddenness, the finality of it all, without the means to respond. No goodbye; nothing. Years of nothing.'

I swatted a fly away that was repeatedly trying to land on my arm.

'Did she have writer's block?' I asked.

Dulcie shook her head quite vehemently at this. 'God, no. Not at all. In fact, she had the opposite. She had

178

writer's … deluge. And in a way that can be just as destructive, for one cannot always effectively judge the standard of the work when it comes pouring out; one merely gets caught up in the mania of it all. And it was mania.'

'Can I ask you something else?'

'You don't need to ask me if you can ask something. Just skip that bit in future, Robert. We'll all be dead soon.'

'Why does Romy call you the "spinner of honey"?'

'Because at that time I had a passion for beekeeping, amongst other things.'

'Here?'

'Yes, here. Until I stopped. Even giving it away, there was still more honey than one person and her dog needs. One spins the comb to extract the honey in liquid form. So Honeyspinner became her name for me. Or one of them, anyway.'

We sat in silence for quite some time, and I considered whether to ask Dulcie one more question. Finally I did.

'Have you ever thought about getting *The Offing* published?'

Dulcie sighed and then squinted out at the sea, which was sparkling. But she said nothing.

'Perhaps it's too painful for you to read.'

She turned and snapped at me then. 'Your problem is you're too astute for one so humble.'

'I'm sorry. I don't know a thing about poetry. But I thought the book was brilliant and that other people might feel the same.'

'There you go again, playing the simple cap-wringing, semi-literate country lad.'

Dulcie caught herself. She straightened herself. Adjusted her hat.

'No, it's me that's sorry, Robert. Don't take my sharp tongue personally. But you shouldn't do yourself down either. The point is, Romy's poetry moved you, so your opinion is as valid as anyone's. In fact, *you* are exactly who she was writing to. The critics she never cared for. Or the academics. Hers was a working-class upbringing too and she just wanted to be read, so she would definitely be delighted to hear your praise, she really would.'

'Weren't you tempted to read the collection, though, Dulcie?'

'Every single day.'

'But you never have.'

'I thought I had made that abundantly clear.'

'Could I ask why?'

'I thought that too would be abundantly clear.'

Dulcie sighed deeply when she saw that I didn't understand how the manuscript – something that might hold answers to her questions – could sit untouched for years, so continued.

'Are you afraid of ghosts?' she asked.

I shook my head. 'I don't believe in them.'

'That's not what I asked.'

Confused, I shook my head again.

'We are all of us afraid of being confronted by our past selves in the small hours of the night,' she said.

'That's what ghosts are: the raw truths we dare not face or the voices of those we have failed. We carry within us our own ghosts with which we haunt ourselves. To read the book would be to raise the dead, and I'm not quite ready for that. And that's all I'll say on the matter.'

'But there are surely others out there like me who would enjoy the poetry collection.'

The conversation clearly closed, Dulcie said nothing and appeared deep in troubled thought, but then her face suddenly brightened and her tone changed entirely.

'Listen, I've had a tremendous idea. You've been working like a Sherpa on that blasted studio and I think I'm suffering a touch of the old cabin fever myself. All this gloomy chat is getting to me so why not let's crank up one of the engines and go for a Sunday drive. And if it's not Sunday, then we shall name it appropriately.'

'What do you mean by "one of the engines"?'

'Well, a motor-car one, of course.'

'You have a car?'

'I have several.'

I was taken aback by this revelation. Aside from the farm vehicles that I had come across, I had never yet met anyone who owned an automobile for what might be termed recreational purposes, let alone several of them. Vehicles were large and dirty and practical – coughing, growling, mud-splattered things – and the thought of someone I knew actually owning a vehicle had never occurred to me. Only the wealthy kept cars.

'But how?'

'What do you mean *how*? I acquired them.'

'All at once?'

'What questions you ask. Of course not.'

For a moment I wondered if perhaps Dulcie was having me on. I looked around.

'But where do you keep them?'

'Well.' She paused for a moment. 'There's one in an underground car park in deepest Chelsea and another is being kept warm by a dear friend who drives it around the lanes of the improbably named village of Upper Slaughter in the Cotswolds, and then there's two – no, wait, three – in a barn at Francis Storm's place.'

'Where is that?'

Dulcie gestured behind her. 'Just up the hill there. The big farm at the top of the land is Frank's. You'll have passed it on the way in. Wait here a minute.'

She rooted around in a drawer in the parlour and returned with a large bunch of keys.

'Let's take the Citroën. You'll have to fetch it, though, I'm afraid. It's the one that is the colour of a bruised aubergine. Or at least it was the last time I looked. One of these keys will do the job.'

'Won't the farmer mind?'

'Mind? It's my bloody car and he gets a nice wedge of rent to spend on pig feed and gumboots, don't you worry.'

'But what if he thinks I'm stealing it and shoots me?'

'You have the keys, don't you?'

'What if he thinks I've burgled your house and taken them?'

'You wouldn't do that. You're a good lad.'

'He doesn't know that.'

'I admire your active imagination but Frank Storm won't care. Trust me. His place is up top. You can't miss it – just follow the smell and then head out back to where the barns are. I believe the Citroën is in the left-hand one. Just have a poke about. On a nice day like this Frank will be out and about anyway: he owns damn near all the way down to Whitby. Take Butler if you're bothered. He can vouch for you.'

'There's just one problem, Dulcie.'

She sighed. 'Yes?'

'I can't drive.'

'Can't drive? You barely even have to.'

'But I can't drive at all.'

'Can anyone really drive?'

'Well, yes.'

'Robert, honestly. It's only two hundred yards away, and it's all downhill. Just take the handbrake off and let it roll down of its own momentum. Plain sailing. All you have to do is steer it around a couple of gentle corners and toot the horn on occasion. Oh, and brake when necessary.'

'But which pedal is the brake?'

'It's the right-hand one. Or maybe it's in the middle. Oh, you'll work it out. There's barely a soul about.' She could see my hesitation. 'Are you fearful?'

'No,' I said, defiantly. 'I'm not scared, me.'

'Good. You fetch the Citroën and I'll fix us a pack-up. Ten minutes will give me just enough time to make a coleslaw to go with the chicken drummers I roasted last night. And a bloody good job I did too. I'd better select a good bottle as well. Or as good as I can muster from my waning batch, anyway. And remember to take the hound – he's a dab old hand at steering. He'll see you right.'

The car hopped forward as if it had a tank full of rabbits when I turned the engine over. It coughed once and then twice, and then kicked into life with a rusty splutter. Though it was a beautifully designed and desirable vehicle, Dulcie's Citroën showed clear signs of suffering from neglect, with spots of rust speckling its sleek flanks and a patina of algae slowly spreading around the rubber seal of the window frames. The wax sheen of its exterior was etched with scuffs and scratches, and a spider had spun an elaborate web in the corner of the windscreen's interior.

A marvellous array of dials sat before me.

I knew that a car was operated by gears so with some force I pushed the stick into first, where it made a guttural, grinding noise, and then I worked the pedals until I found that by pressing one and releasing the other the car hopped forward again. Then the engine went dead. The car peeked from the barn's entrance by about three inches.

I started it up and nudged forward again, smoother this time, the cold hard tyres crunching across warm gravel, then slowly turned the large wheel to steer this mass of metal and leather through Frank Storm's farmyard.

I was driving, *very slowly.*

But I was nonetheless driving.

As I dipped through divots in the ground and gripped the wheel too tightly, I pushed open the window. A well-fed cat with green eyes appeared from an adjacent barn to walk alongside the car for a few moments, but it soon got bored as it overtook me and then cut across my path.

'Haven't had a single lesson,' I called after it. It momentarily turned to cast me a withering look of disdain that is solely the preserve of the semi-feral farm cat. 'Not one,' I added.

The car rolled out of the yard and I turned into the road and let gravity take over. As Dulcie had remarked, it was all down a fairly steep hill and even in first gear I started to pick up a decent pace. This driving lark was easy. As easy as licking monkey's blood syrup from an ice cream. I let one hand dangle out of the window and wiggled my fingers in the breeze.

It was a feeling of complete, unfettered freedom.

Something shot across the road, low and dark, from the cover of one earthen bankside to the other. It was low-scuttling but fast-moving – a stoat or a weasel, perhaps. Was there a difference? I slammed on the brakes without knowing which pedal exactly operated the brakes. Instead the car lurched forward with a growl like a sleeping dog poked with a stick, and then a louder, more urgent roar that saw the pointers on several of the dials jump in unison, and in my panic I overcompensated with the wheel, veering first one way and then the other to briefly mount the grassy verge, where, for a long, lingering second, it felt as if I might tip the car over entirely. Somehow I got back on course, though, and the road wound downwards, carving around tight bends that I took with ease. I was gliding now, the towering ancient hedgerows flashing by in a blur with snatched glimpses through the gateway gaps at the fields that lay behind them, then suddenly the left turn into Dulcie's dead-end lane was upon me. I bore down and took it tight without braking.

The smooth tarmac gave way to the rough dirt track full of ruts and dried-up puddle holes. I leaned to one side as the car fishtailed in the dust, a billowing plume behind me as I bounced and crashed down the track. The spider's web vibrated and the glove compartment fell open, spilling a mess of empty cigarette packets, a pair of gloves and a half-drunk bottle of spirits onto the floor. I slapped the wheel with my hot palms, exhilarated. The end of the lane and the meadow were fast approaching so I hit one pedal and nothing happened. I tried another and the car accelerated. I tried the third, hard, and it slammed the car to a standstill right outside the cottage at the precise moment that Dulcie casually stepped out of the back door, sporting a racing-green-coloured cape that draped down to just an inch or two above the settling dust. It was fastened across her breast by a large pin decorated with what appeared to be the eye from a peacock's plumage.

I had stalled again. The engine was dead.

'Ah,' said Dulcie. 'Excellent.'

I was still in first gear.

With Butler and an oversized hamper strapped in the back, Dulcie drove us extremely slowly – though not as slowly as I had – up the steep single road that led inland, away from the bay. All the windows were wound down to clear the car of its decidedly musty odour.

'We'll head for the moors while I get my bearings,' she said, hunched over the wheel as she tried various switches and levers. 'Now, my eyes would shame a myopic mole so what I want you to do, Robert, is shout up if you see me drifting across the road. Shout loudly. Will you do that?'

We rose up out of the lower lands and, as we crested a steep peak in the road, without warning Dulcie suddenly accelerated and I felt the omelette leap in my stomach.

'The knack is back,' she shouted over the roar of the engine and the wind. She accelerated again. 'I think I should like to see the moors in full summer bloom.'

The road levelled out and took us through miles of moorland billowing in all directions, and we dipped and bounced over undulations and potholes. The dog stuck his head out of the window, his tongue and ears flapping and his lips peeling back to give the impression of a smile.

'This a Citroën Traction Avant,' she shouted, 'which translates as "front-wheel drive", though in France they call it *Reine de la Route*. "Queen of the Road". I rather like that.'

'How old is it?'

'It was one of the first models off the production line – 1934.'

'Did you know Romy then?'

'Only just. Would you believe it if I told you that we met that very day, and she helped me pick it out? It's true. We were drunk and she was very persuasive. The salesman couldn't believe his luck. He was so grateful for his first sale that he gave me free driving gloves and a bottle of fake champagne, which tasted like horse piss but we had finished it by the time we got home nonetheless.'

Here the road forked and at the very last moment Dulcie jerked the car to the right, and all contents that weren't strapped down slid in the opposite direction.

Soon we were driving down into the village of Grosmont, but Dulcie did not slow, not for a moment, and in a shot we had left it behind and just a few minutes later were speeding through Goathland with a honk of the horn that disturbed the stillness of the village green, and a man stepped out of the post office to stare, agog, as if we were at the helm of an invading Panzer rather than a mud-splattered, sleek-looking Citroën driven by a waving, whooping tall lady and a dog happily trailing long strings of drool the length of the village.

In time we entered trees and twice Dulcie pointed and shouted, but her words were lost in the noise of movement, and though I was slightly afraid that she might crash the car I did my best not to show it. The stench of petrol was strong as we drove deep into the thick forest where pines towered and loomed on either side, and I caught glimpses between the columns of timber of cool, dry clearings carpeted with the thick weft of dead needles upon which shafts of sunlight fell, and occasionally there were fleeting gaps in which road signs pointed to tiny villages where woodsmen lived and worked.

The trees ended and a back road took us into a town that was busy with people on market day, and Dulcie was forced to slow. She leaned in close and shouted in an unnecessarily loud voice, 'Pickering: full of crusty old duffers, best press on', and she floored the car again, accelerating at such speed that several cars pulled over to let us past or slowed in order to remonstrate, their drivers angrily waving their fists.

Signs for other places flashed by.

Kirby Misperton. Amotherby.

Scagglethorpe. Brawby.

We skirted the town of Malton and then a few minutes later Dulcie finally slowed and took a right turn onto a long road that appeared impossibly straight, and which ran like a ribbon into the heart of a great private country estate. We passed beneath the arches of an ornate gatehouse, followed the road to an obelisk on a roundabout, and then turned right again onto a drive that led to the biggest house I had ever seen, perhaps the biggest in Britain, a beautiful sprawling palace of stone with a huge domed roof and wings running off to either side, and walled gardens, and acre upon acre of green lawns leading down to a lake.

'Well, now,' said Dulcie. 'Not a bad little pile.'

Everywhere I looked there was opulence and architectural grandeur designed to evoke feelings of such awe and wonder that it forced me to reconsider my sense of perspective.

'Where are we?'

'Castle Howard, domicile of the Howard family since the first foundations were dug in 1699, though of course it is rather ostentatious to call it a castle when it is, in fact, merely a very large stately house – though, granted, an ambitious effort that incorporates several different styles: a bit of baroque here, a touch of Palladian over there.'

'Do people *live* here?'

'Certainly.'

'In all that space?'

'In all that space.'

Dulcie pulled off the road and steered us down onto the vast lawn. She turned off the engine and when the car rolled to a stop she got out. Butler jumped out beside her.

'A fine spot for a snack, I'd say.'

I climbed out and looked at the tyre tracks we had left across the pristine grass.

'Do you know the owners?' I asked.

'No. Should I?'

'I just thought it might be a bit odd for them to find some strangers pitching up in their garden.'

'Like you pitching up in my garden, you mean?'

I realised she had me there, and could offer no reply.

'Come on and help me with this,' she said as she cast her cape aside and unfolded a tartan picnic rug.

Dulcie drove with less urgency on the return journey. Nips from a hip flask containing a liquid that gave her teeth a deep red tint, along with the food and the excitement of the drive down, had combined to make her somewhat lethargic as we headed east this time, leaving the Howardian Hills.

We bypassed Malton once more and took the Scarborough road across the Vale of Pickering through mile upon mile of open countryside whose vast open spaces were punctuated by numerous small villages, many of them split between East and West or Lower and Upper, in which there were family lines that had barely strayed beyond these small communities where farming was the main occupation and where there was little work to be had that didn't concern agriculture. Others bore the names of past cultures – of further Viking settlements established by raiding parties: Staxton, Flixton – the language of the land joining to create a narrative through shifting epochs and changing rulers. Yet for those who tilled and turned the soil, and harvested the land's bounty at summer's end, here life had stayed relatively constant for centuries, with existence spare and closely tied to the changing seasons.

All around us war had left a stain, and the shape of rural life was changing. Rationing had created an appetite that was proving to be insatiable and farm plots were being bought up and reconfigured for mass production. Hunger rather than conflict was the great fear now. The days of the simple ox and the plough that my father had spoken of were long over.

We drove through the suburban fringes of Scarborough, gliding down side streets of tall town houses advertising vacancies, and after catching fleeting views of the early evening sea, drove inland and back up onto the moors, for no one had seen fit to lay a road on this wild stretch of prehistoric coastline that led back to a bay whose appeal was in its isolation, accessible as it was only by those strong in thigh, sturdy of boat or keen in wonder.

As she drove, Dulcie's chin slumped ever closer to the steering wheel and twice I loudly instigated conversation to ensure that she was awake, and each time she turned her head and looked at me as if I were a stranger, confused and bleary-eyed as if pulled back from the precipice of a deep sleep.

She spoke little, and her demeanour was one of deflation.

The dog detected as much and by the time we pulled down the narrow uneven lane that led to her cottage he was licking at Dulcie Piper's earlobe from the back seat. She parked the car haphazardly and left Butler and me to our own devices as she sullenly headed into the house without a word.

IX

I didn't swim that evening. Instead I spent the night with the verses of John Clare. Of all the poems that Dulcie had impressed upon me, his were the ones with which I felt the greatest affinity. Some of his work – those pieces that documented his wanderings down the lanes and across the fields of England, observing the seasons, working, pursuing freedom – was like a mirror held up to my own life. Until then I hadn't realised that there existed such poets who laboured on the land and wrote down what they saw and felt, what they smelled and tasted and heard.

Up until that summer, poetry had been a secret code spoken only by toffs, as mystifying as the Latin they seemed so fond of quoting. It had been just one more way of keeping the working men and women in their place, a locked-out world of lives never to be lived by the likes of me. Poetry had been a way of complicating the simple.

Yet I now found that secret universe opening up to me a little more each night through poems read in the studio, and nowhere more so than in the words of John Clare, agricultural worker and prophet of the soil, written more than century earlier. The strength of feeling he conveyed was almost overwhelming and I especially returned to one work, an epic in miniature called 'The Flitting', which resonated deeply and which I attempted to memorise in substantial chunks of rhyming verse. This breathless display of microcosmic poetic cartography – of rabbit tracks and molehills, hawthorn hedges and orchard floors, of nightingales and crooked stiles – was one that I too was experiencing. Clare was a new friend and confidant, a spirit guide and voice of comfort in the lamplit shadows of this creaking shelter.

And still each night I thought of the girls on the beach. No matter how much physical labour or swimming I had done during the day, they distracted me to the point of insomnia.

My head whirled and my fizzy blood swirled and popped in my ears as I lay back and thought of their thighs and their flat stomachs. I thought of the backs of their knees, their nostrils and the wrinkles of their elbows. I wondered how their hair must smell when it was wet and how often they cut their toenails. I thought of whether they put sugar in their tea and what their armpits looked like and the different ways in which they walked on the wet sand and whether they had tasted lobster and collected fossils or coloured their hair or read John Clare.

And I wondered what thoughts kept them awake at night.

This preoccupation with the girls of the bay made me want to learn to write so that I could compose poems to all of them and then leave those poems folded into cracks in the rocks for the tide to take, the ink washing free of the paper, the paper slowly mashing to a pulp, the pulp joining all the other decaying matter in the great slate-grey soup, and then – and only then – would I have the courage to tell them that they were the subjects of great poems, but to read those poems they must learn to read the sea. Then, hearing these words, and understanding my honest intentions, and recognising the poetry of such a romantic gesture, perhaps then they would fall for me entirely.

But until that day came I continued to lie in the dark on the creaking floorboards with the night wrapped around me and my legs restlessly twitching with desire; I felt a sort of illiterate emotional helplessness over the impossibility of any of this ever happening. These outcomes existed only in the white-burning pit of my sunstroked imagination, and in the morning I awoke, itching, sweaty and encrusted to the coarse wool of my blankets.

I had only just dozed off when I heard a noise. A moan of anguish. I lay still, searching for its origin in the flat and endless silence, and then there it was again. A muffled wail, coming from the cottage. I pulled on my boots and went to the edge of the meadow, and stood looking at the house. The night was cool and unmoving. Once more I heard it – a wail, and then a sob, followed by the bulb of Dulcie's bedroom being switched on to cast flat panels of light across the garden.

I ducked down, afraid of the embarrassment of being spotted lurking without explanation. The light stayed on for several minutes so I returned to my sleeping bag and blankets, my lower legs wet with dew, for one final reading of 'The Flitting'.

> She feels a love for little things
> That very few can feel beside
> And still the grass eternal springs
> Where castles stood and grandeur died.

I drifted off in 1833 and slept for a century or more.

The day was still and dry so I spent the morning working on the final task in the studio's restoration: painting the outside with a double coat of whitewash. I had already sanded the coarse old wooden panels down so that the last remaining flakes of the previous layer had been removed, and now I slapped on the paint thick and fast.

Soon the transformation was nearly complete, the previously dejected-looking structure that I had found hunkered down in the meadow's corner, rotting like a storm-felled oak, appearing to stand straight and true now, somehow prouder of itself, its reset window frames impervious to the elements, the scabrous roof tiles scrubbed of cloying moss and free from leaks, and its interior entirely fixed up and ready for habitation again. I had sorted through those possessions in there that Dulcie wished to keep and got rid of the remaining refuse of rancid rags, broken furniture, spent light bulbs and so forth. I had fixed the toilet cistern and even installed a new liner for the chimney flue so that the old wood-burning stove, once soot-stained and ineffective, but now polished up and in pristine condition, had such a strong draw on it that, within minutes of lighting a small pyre of kindling and a couple of long-seasoned logs, it was emitting more than enough heat to turn the studio sauna-like on a warm summer's day.

I painted for several hours and when the first coat was beginning to dry I added a second coat until landing flies became trapped there; my hair and torso were flecked with pinhead spots of white paint and my arms ached, and I found myself parched with thirst.

I called for Dulcie at the house but she did not respond. I heard only Butler scratching somewhat frantically at the inside of the door. When I opened it he bolted past me and straight into the meadow, sprinting with intent as if tracking the scent of a fox that had had the temerity to stray across his patch in daylight hours.

I followed the movement of the long grass as, hidden, he carved a trail down beyond the tangle of scrub at the bottom end where I had experienced what I could only describe as a reverie or waking hallucination during that first day in this strange and magical corner of the countryside. I picked up my pace and very nearly stumbled headlong into the sunken spring tucked between tussocks of grass, only just managing to adjust my footing and shift my centre of gravity at the last moment.

There was a shape beneath the brambles. A prone figure down in the shadows.

Butler reached her first and I arrived a moment later, gasping for breath, trickles of sweat running down my temples.

It was Dulcie.

She was lying on her side as if in the recovery position, and I saw that her hands were drenched with what appeared to be blood. It was smeared on her face too – a streak of it was around her mouth and one red fingerprint was imprinted on a cheek. Her wide-brimmed hat was beside her.

Gulping for air, I froze. The dog whined and gently ducked down beneath the brambles, and proceeded to tenderly lap at her face.

All of a sudden Dulcie was awake, animated again.

'Urgh. What *are* you doing?'

She swatted the dog away, and then looked at me, slightly puzzled. She slowly lifted herself up onto one elbow.

'Don't try to move,' I said.

'Why the devil not?'

'You're hurt.'

'Am I?'

'Yes – there's blood.'

I pointed at her hands. Dulcie looked at them for a moment and then belched, long and low, and then made some noises of mastication. She smacked her lips and reached for her hat.

'Oh, you are so unnecessarily dramatic, Robert. Honestly.'

'I thought something had happened.'

'Blackberries happened. Too many of them. They've come up early and are still a bit tart but a sprinkle of muscovado should take the edge off them. I'll cook them down, make a jam. Or I thought perhaps a nice cool compote. I'm afraid I taste-tested one too many.'

'I thought – '

'What? That I'd snuffed it?'

Dulcie whooped with delight.

'I saw you on the ground.'

'Yes, having a nap, as I have seen you yourself do on several occasions.'

She laughed again, louder this time.

'It's not funny,' I said.

'It bloody *is*. Now, help me up, will you.'

We slowly walked back to the cottage, with Butler beside us.

'I suppose down there with the worms wouldn't be the worst way to go,' said Dulcie, philosophically.

We pushed through the grass, the sea at our backs.

'I hope you don't mind me asking, Dulcie, but I thought I heard a noise last night.'

'That's not a question. It's a statement.'

'Was it you I heard?'

'I don't know. What did you hear?'

'A sort of upset wailing.'

'Probably foxes. At it.'

'Coming from your house.'

She didn't look at me.

'Then it must have been Butler. He's prone to sleep-talking. Dogs do it, you know. They're perfectly capable.'

Still she looked away, over to the studio, which was a gleaming white cube drying in the midday sun.

'It sounded more like – '

'Kippers,' interrupted Dulcie. 'I thought we could have kippers so smoky that you'd swear they were dredged from the ashes of a bonfire. We'll also have one perfectly poached egg apiece, or perhaps two or more for you as it seems that you have been busy. Consider it the world's tardiest prepared breakfast, but to make up for it I shall segue quite quickly into a very early afternoon tea of scones as big as your fist to go with the compote. But – oh, buck and fugger. I've just remembered we're lacking clotted cream. Scones without proper cream is a disaster of apocalyptic proportions.'

'Now who is being unnecessarily dramatic. It sounds more than enough as it is.'

'In return for the spread I ask just one small favour.'

'Of course. What is it, Dulcie?'

We were back at her garden fence, standing on the patch I had freed of weeds, but which was already being pulled back by the meadow again. I had lost track of how long it had been since I scythed a passage through it.

'If the mood takes us later, perhaps you might read me one poem.'

'Any poem?'

'From *The Offing*.'

I hesitated.

'Well, yes. If you would like me to. It would be a privilege.'

'Good. Now you should go and wash your hands. The kippers and accompaniments will be served in seven minutes or less.' She scratched behind the dog's ears. 'Fish skin for afters, noble beast,' she said to him. 'Your favourite.'

———

Later, when I returned from my evening swim to burn off the double-portioned feast of the afternoon, the outside table was set with a circle of candles of different heights and colours, their flames flickering in the gentle sea breeze of the settling evening.

'How was the water?'

'Wet and wonderful,' I replied as I towelled the final dampness from my hair. 'Should I get the poems now?'

She nodded. 'I'll fetch a bottle. There's a brandy I've been saving for an occasion, though I never imagined it would be for this. I fear I shall need it.'

Dulcie was lighting a very large cigar with a match that was dwarfed beside it when I came back with the manuscript. She was taking short, sharp draws on it until it was fully ignited, and then she tossed the match aside and exhaled a long heavy plume of thick smoke, followed by a small cough. I had never seen a woman smoking a cigar before; rarely had I seen a man smoke one either. The miners in the village favoured either filterless Capstans or sometimes took pipes during their brief leisure time on a Sunday. Cigars were symbols for things most would never know: wealth and opulence.

'I didn't know you smoked, Dulcie.'

'Only with poetry.'

I sat down. She took from her pocket a large brass ashtray, which was in the shape of a fly whose wings pivoted upwards to reveal a compartment inside, and she carefully tapped ash into it.

'Which one would you like me to read?'

'How could I choose when I don't know its contents? I thought we had established that there's a reason it has lain untouched, gathering dust.'

'Maybe I should pick one at random.'

Dulcie puffed on her cigar and poured me two fingers of brandy. I was wearing my one clean shirt.

'Maybe you should be less decisive.'

'I'm not too sure about that,' I replied.

I thumbed through the manuscript and chanced upon a poem entitled 'Threnody for the Drowned'.

'What's a threnody, Dulcie?'

She exhaled smoke. A veil of it rose over her face until she wafted it away.

'It is almost certainly a word that Romy would use, that's what. It means a song that is sung in mourning. Or a poem. A lament for the deceased.' She cleared her throat before continuing. 'One might even describe it as a wail.'

'Oh,' I said, suddenly understanding more than I had expected.

She continued. 'Without reading it, I think we can assume that this particular work was a foreshadowing of events that followed – a warning to the world, though of course the world never got a chance to heed it.'

'A cry for help?'

'Rather a statement of intent.'

I took a sip of the brandy. It tasted like pure fire. Dire. I drank some more.

'Maybe I'll read another one instead.'

'It's your choice. But tell me – I'm curious – what is the opening line of that poem?'

'"Blossoms of blood / flower then flood",' I read. 'No, I think I'll choose another one.'

I looked through the contents. Dulcie's cigar had gone out, and she struck another match to light it.

'I think this one is about you,' I said.

She noisily sucked on the cigar as she went through the elaborate routine of getting it going until the heavy bitter smoke was billowing thick around us once again.

'I'll be the judge of that. Let the seance begin.'

'It's called "The Honeyspinner".'

She shook the match out.

'Oh.'

I proceeded to read it just as it was on the page.

The Honeyspinner

Your breath arrives across
the pillow, a savannah breeze.

Your mouth has produced
no tumbleweeds

while you were sleeping.
And while you were sleeping.

The ravenous wolves have been
cast from the kingdom of cruelty

and outside the first sweet drops
of morning rain fall

like a drunk violinist on the steps
of the marble cenotaph.

When I finished, Dulcie took a large gulp of brandy and then poured more.

'Read it again, please. A little more slowly this time.'

She closed her eyes. I took a sip of my drink and then did as she requested.

Dulcie said nothing for a long time. The cigar sat smouldering between her fingers. It hung there, a ribbon of blue smoke drifting across the garden and into the meadow. I noticed then bats flitting across the grass, ducking and darting as they gorged on the evening's insects.

'Yes,' she said, her eyes still closed. 'Yes.'

I drained my glass. The brandy didn't taste so bad once you got used to it. There was a burnt fruitiness beneath it, an aftertaste that lingered long beyond the final gulped drops.

'Just one more time.'

I read it again, and when it was over Dulcie opened her eyes.

'My God. She was a genius.'

She poured us both another brandy and we sat watching as the bats scoured the sky.

Finally Dulcie broke the silence of nightfall's exuberant theatrics. 'You know what you want to do? You want to get yourself a girlfriend.'

Her voice was elongated by the alcohol and a slight slurring was making her words bleed into one another.

When I didn't reply, Dulcie added: 'Or a boyfriend. Or one of each. Treat yourself.' Again, when I didn't respond, she circled her glass in the air and asked: 'Is there anyone back at home?'

I screwed my face up. Embarrassed to be broaching the subject, I shook my head. 'Anyone worth bothering with wouldn't bother with me.'

'You're underselling yourself, Robert.'

'All the lasses round my way are daft.'

Again she circled her glass and this time brandy swirled around its rim and splashed onto her wrist.

'Then you need to cast your net further afield. Which you are doing already, I suppose, just by being here. Yes, cast your net and reel it in. The fisherman doesn't wait for the fish to jump out of the sea and into his boat. He goes out to the spawning grounds.'

'I'm not really looking.'

'Not even a peek?'

Dulcie looked at me sideways with the faintest of smiles.

Trying not to smile back, I shrugged.

'Not even a glance at one of the diggers down bay for the day, or at the fresh-faced and strapping farm girls driven in from the moors on their fathers' tractors while they're off selling ewes over Egton way?'

Despite her crisp and correct English accent, and the nullifying effect of the drink, I noticed that Dulcie pronounced 'ewes' the Yorkshire way – 'yows'.

'Maybe a glance,' I conceded.

'Of course you do. You're a young man full of blood and all the rest of it. When I was your age I'd – ' She hesitated, looked away. Took a sip. 'Well, we'll not get into that.'

Now my interest was piqued. 'What had you done by my age, Dulcie?'

She raised her glass to her lips but spoke before it reached them.

'I'd scandalised the local vicar's daughter, that's what. I was thrown out of school for that, and thank Christ I was. Because if there is a hell on earth then it is surely an English boarding school attended by the dimwit debutante spawn of diplomats, aristocrats, old-money dilettantes and those jug-eared, buck-toothed royals who flounce about flaunting their family names as flagrantly as their crests and signet rings.'

'What did you do?'

'With Verity?'

'No, after you were kicked out?'

'I began to live, Robert. And to love too. And that is what you must do. Live and love as many mouths, hands and clammy holes as you can cram yourself into, and then, when you find someone who satisfies your soul too, you give yourself to them entirely.'

She sniffed at her drink and then finally took a sip.

'Pleasure is not a crime,' she said. 'It's a birthright.'

The brandy's punishment was a dull and insistent pain in my head the following morning. I awoke early but could not move, not even for water, and instead lay still as the sun crept across the walls of the studio, and the floorboards groaned and creaked as they warmed up, hard beneath my back. Around me the meadow was waking after a short night devoid of true darkness. It was high summer now. The deepest part of it, when life was peaking in blossoming bouquets of green, and the sap had risen, and even the sea was a true green. It appeared broader now, less of a barrier somehow and more an extension of the rolling land that crept towards it – and beneath it – like a mattress beside a jumbled pile of khaki blankets. I saw a fly overhead. It moved with jerking angular motions, as if drawing squares in the air above me. I went back to sleep and dreamed of great clouds of flies and then the sea closing in over my head, and the muted roar and rumble of its underwater music.

I heard my name being called. It was Dulcie, from around the far side of the cottage. I pulled on my clothes and boots and stepped out into a day so bright I had to take a moment to let my eyes adjust as the glare pressed hot shapes onto my retinas.

I saw Dulcie urgently waving her arms, as if drowning in the roily swell of jade.

When she caught my attention she too shaded her eyes with a forearm and pointed with the other hand to the fence just beyond the lean-to, where the narrow copse that clung to the tiny hillside stream began.

I hurried over. 'What is it?'

'A swarm.' She seemed excited.

'What?'

'Bees. A pother of them, just settled – look.'

I followed the line of her finger to a low-hanging branch from which there hung a pendulous swarm, the shape of a teardrop.

'*Apis mellifera*,' she said. 'The European honey bee. Bloody hundreds of them. What luck.'

'Luck?'

'Yes. It is surely a sign, is it not? I rather suspect this is nature's way of subtly suggesting that I might want to get back into the old honey racket again – with your help, that is.'

I looked back to the branch where the bees were clambering over one another, a seething febrile shifting shape of legs and wings.

'But I don't know the first thing about beekeeping.'

'You don't need to – you've got me. I'll be the brains and you can be the brawn, as it were. And Butler can watch from a safe distance. He is embittered by past traumatic experiences. He got thrice stung up the scut, you see. He went into a kind of trance. It was most peculiar.'

The dog was indeed well out of the way, only his large head and ears visible from the cottage's porch.

'I had to pick the stings out,' Dulcie added wistfully.

I did not move. The collective hum of the swarm was, to me, a malevolent one; I had been stung enough times to know the pain bees could inflict. A sting on the thin, fat-free skin of the scalp was particularly bad, like a hammer blow.

'What do we do?'

'Precisely nothing for now. We let them settle in for a nice little rest after an arduous journey, then when their hands are behind their heads and they're wiggling their toes we'll scoop them up and give them a nice new home. The rent will be minimal: a little honey paid to us now and then, as and when.'

'Where will they stay?'

'In one of the hives, of course.'

'Which hives?'

'My old bee metropolis down at the bottom of the meadow, by the brambles. Haven't you seen them?'

While Dulcie busied herself with preparations, I hastily cleared the patch of brambles, and sure enough there were half-a-dozen old hives in the undergrowth. I made just enough space to access the nearest one, removed the lid and then removed the frames one by one, as Dulcie had instructed, and then carried them back to hose them. She appeared with a sheet, a cardboard box, secateurs and a small piece of wood.

'This will do it.'

'How will you get them in there?'

'How will *you* get them in there, I think you mean. Here. Put this on.' She passed me a white beekeeper's suit.

'But what if they get angry?'

'You'll be fine. Just stand still and stay calm. Or step into the shade – bees rarely bother you in the shade.'

'Really?'

She shrugged. 'Probably. Just remember you're bigger than them.'

'But you're bigger than me,' I countered.

'Exactly – and I'm not afraid of you, so you shouldn't be of them. Now go and welcome our new neighbours. There's the entire population of an entire bee city just awaiting a new honey factory to occupy.'

'I might get stung.'

'Yes, you might.'

'But doesn't it hurt?'

'The taste of the honey soon makes you forget that. Anyway, you're probably thinking of wasps. And if they didn't sting we might as well be boxing up bluebottles, and where's the fun in that? Look: the scout bees are doing a waggle dance. They must have been out searching for a new home. The timing is perfect. I'll instruct you.'

I reluctantly stepped into the suit and Dulcie helped affix the mesh-masked headpiece. She stood back and surveyed me. 'Yes, that'll do. How do you feel in there?'

'Trapped.'

'Ah, but it bears repeating: nothing tastes as good as honey made by bees that feed on the heather of the North Yorkshire moors, Robert. You'll see. Trust me. I'd trade a ton of steak tartare and a barrowload of beluga for a jar or two of homespun honey. Do you know why?'

'Because you like eating?'

'Because honey is liquid poetry. It's like a slice of sun spread on your bread. It's the very essence of the natural world – of land and insect and man, or woman, working in perfect harmony. Bees are wonders, they really are, the way they motor along, turning pollen into gold. And the harmonious organisation of their societies is something we can surely learn from: "From their bellies comes / a drink of varying colours / containing healing for mankind." Do you know who said that?'

Distracted, I pulled on the protective gloves. 'Was it your friend Lawrence?'

'Not even close. It's from the Qur'an, written a good deal earlier than that most holy of bibles – though I prefer to call it the Holy *Bibble* – and only a marginally less dry read, though both need a damn good editor. Here – ' She passed me the secateurs. 'Right, then. These bees won't box themselves.'

I edged over to the pendulous, crawling mass and when I turned back I saw that Dulcie had moved further away and from this safe distance was urging me forward with gestures. Beads of sweat gathered on my brow and at my temples. Still haunted by memories of being stung in unexpected places, Butler too had retreated even further.

'I thought you said they were harmless,' I said, my voice rising slightly.

'You're the one in the safety suit. Besides, a lad of your size, it would take between one and one and a half thousand stings to kill you.'

'Is that true?'

She ignored my question, a habit that I had noticed she resorted to when she couldn't confirm the veracity of these bold declarations.

'Now, all you need to do is carefully snip the branch to which they cling and then lower the whole lot into that cardboard box,' Dulcie instructed. 'It'll be quite heavy, I'm sure, but I see that the summer has at least put some meat on your lean bones.'

I moved closer and the swarm seemed to stir at my approach, but rather than seeing it as one insidious humming mass I instead considered the bees as individuals, each one a tiny cog in the machinery of the collective.

'Remember,' said Dulcie, 'no bee wants to harm you any more than you do it.'

'I don't want to harm them at all.'

'Exactly my point.'

I reached out and cut the branch. Several bees took flight, but many stray ones appeared to re-join the shifting, quietly buzzing entity that I held before me. It was quite beautiful.

'That's it. That's it.'

'Your commentary is distracting,' I said out of the side of my mouth.

'Listen to them sing. Listen to the music they make.'

Dulcie was practically dancing with delight, yet all I could hear was a low, scratchy hum. A dry drone. I lowered the branch into the box.

'Gently does it, now, Robert. Treat it as if it were a newborn child being delivered into the world.'

'I don't know how to deliver a child,' I said, this time through gritted teeth.

'Then apply some basic common sense, for God, Muhammad and Satan's sake.'

I put the bees into the box.

'What do I do now?'

'Place the box on the ground and cover it with this.' She tossed me the sheet.

'Right,' said Dulcie. 'Good. Now we only have to – '

'I like that you continue to use the word "we".'

'And I like that you're finally learning to answer back. That's good. You're finally getting some vinegar in your piss. All *we* have to do is flip the whole thing arse-about-tit and wedge it open an inch with a branch or stick.'

'Won't they escape?'

'Robert, the bees aren't prisoners – the whole point is that they are free to come and go of their own accord. I could never entrap a creature. Never. Not a bird or a goldfish, and even the chickens Romy and I kept had free run of the place. No, the intention is that, happy in their temporary digs, they will emit pheromone signals of such delight that their kith and kin will be alerted as one might be to a house-warming party by formal invitation. By this evening they'll be joined by multitudes. Consider it a hotel, if you must continue to anthropomorphise the critters – and a four-star one off Mayfair, at the very least.'

I followed Dulcie's instructions and was surprised to see that very few bees did indeed leave the box.

'Congratulations,' she said. 'You are now an apiarist. Do you know, in old folklore it was always considered lucky for bees to be kept in partnership; many believed one should never be the sole owner of a hive, and a husband and wife weren't considered much better. In fact, an unattached man and woman were said to be the perfect apiarists. And here's another, even more pertinent fact: a few years back the Ministry of Agriculture began to allow an extra ration of sugar for us beekeepers – ten pounds per colony, as I recall. The thing is, during the war some enterprising wags started siphoning off the sugar for themselves and their families – and rightly so – so then the ministry began to colour the bee rations green and soon enough the bees started to produce green honey. Have you ever heard anything so absurd?'

'Not until I met you, no.'

'Right, then. Lunch.'

On those rare days when I woke to a sky the colour of stone, and the sea was a turbid mass of foul and foaming cream, and there was a nip in the air, or clodded clouds were folding themselves into furrowed peaks to the far blurred line of the offing, I forsook my usual ocean swim or morning dip in the stream for a different cleansing routine. Instead I rose early and walked down to the far end of the meadow, where the land dipped and the wild grass grew thick, each blade heavy with cuckoo spittle, and making sure that I could not be seen, I stripped off and lay down in the coarse carpet. I then rolled this way and that, like a dog, like a baby, making sure that my body was soaked and scratched by the rough grass, pulling out clumps and using them to scrub those parts that needed scrubbing the most. It was an enlivening routine, one that left me feeling prickled but pristine, as polished as a pearl lifted from an oyster shell.

Once or twice I even bathed there at night, with a bar of soap just as white as the moonlight that illuminated the hollow in which I wriggled and writhed, a feral beast momentarily relaxed in the safety of his staked territory, a perfectly wild creature at play.

At times like this, or when hoeing soil or sanding wood, or just sitting on a bench with my face turned to the sun, I appeared to slip out of the moment so entirely – or, conversely, perhaps was so deeply immersed in the here and now – that I forgot who I was. The slate of self was wiped. Gone were all thoughts of past and present, of the stale air of classrooms and of looming exam results, coal boards and pitheads and pension plans, as all worries and concerns were diluted away to nothingness and I drifted in and out of the day, brought back into being only when either the sky or my stomach rumbled, or birdsong broke the silence.

These were lingering states in which I was happy to revel, as night replaced day and day replaced night, and time became not a linear thing but something more elastic, stretching and contracting at will, one minute expanding into a day, one week gone in the blink of an eye. Petals unfolded, willow blossom took to the breeze and hogweed stems grew towering in the shaded dell at the bottom of the meadow, and time itself was measured only by the clock of green growth, and marked out by the simple routine of working, eating, swimming, sleeping.

———

As the balmy evenings extended, Butler found himself being taken on walks of ever-increasing distances. On some nights it felt as if my blood were fizzing with energy, and when it did I headed up to the moors or down bay, past where the houses ended, and along the beach amongst the bedded banks of seaweed, until the village was nothing but a dot behind me, and the hill-side beyond faded in the gloom until I finally turned back to walk home, sweating, parched and exhausted, the path lit only by the radiant moon.

More days and nights passed this way as the season glided onwards and farmers spoke of the driest spell in decades, and I embraced slothfulness in the full heat.

Summer peaked.

And each evening a new poem. With the bees ensconced in their new hive home, the studio's renovations more or less complete and as much order in the meadow as could be imposed, I spent several free days swimming and then exploring the cliffs above, to which there ran a series of steep and narrow wooded vales that were beautifully cool in muggy weather, or I wandered the smugglers' alleyways of the bay itself. I entertained few thoughts about leaving the place. Time stood still; the calendar had been tossed to the turning tides. It was summer, and it felt as if it probably always would be. I would have bet good money against it ever ending.

After every evening meal, loose with the wine that I was getting a taste for, or oiled by the brandy that Dulcie consumed as if it were water, a freshly snipped cigar held between her fingers, I read a single poem from *The Offing*. With each reading I began to slowly gain a greater understanding of this woman that she had loved. Dulcie's responses to the pieces, meanwhile, varied wildly, from disquiet to excitement, from visible grief to impassive silence, yet the next night she was always ready to receive another, just the one, to be savoured. Or perhaps that was all that her emotions would allow. It was difficult to tell, for though I was beginning to learn her strange ways, such as her linguistic dexterity, her distaste for all forms of authority and, of course, her heroic tolerance for alcohol, she seemed unknowable. A part of her was held back – that solid centre that is the irrefutable core of each and every one of us. The self.

There was only one poem from the collection, as far as I could ascertain, that was not set around the bay, and was instead composed in Italy, and even then it explored similar and now-familiar themes, and incorporated the same images that recurred again and again throughout the collection.

'That was written on our final trip together, shortly before all the silly bastards started battling,' said Dulcie by way of explanation. 'We went from Naples to wander the ruins of Pompeii, then on to Sorrento, Positano and all along the Amalfi Coast. It was a holiday, for once, rather than a working trip. What a joy it was to travel Europe and feel part of something greater, to connect with those ancient civilisations that led us to today. Romy's black veil was descending then, and death was surely watching her from around corners and on clifftops, and in her nightmares too, but I do believe there were at least brief moments of sheer happiness during those three weeks. I have to believe that. I have to.'

Amalfi, 1939

White gulls swoop with sirens in their gullets,
their shadow shapes passing over sunken mountain ranges.

Cliffs like cremation curtains drape over lapping waters
and a clear sky catches the hot cough of sleeping Vesuvius.

A distant empty tanker sallies forth for Saudi oil
as breeze patterns play across a surface of shattered jade

and nebulous forms shapeshift in the sea's flooded cellar.
Centreless, lacking skeletons, as broad as mastodons,

they rise from the deep to skim the spring-warmed shallows,
held in a moment by the flashbulb of the unblinking sun,

glimpsed like Ahab's quarry before sinking to mythology,
sunken ghosts stalking the overhangs of the torrid mind.

And down at the harbour wall gannets gather
to peck at the eye of a brilliant gulping turbot.

And Europe holds her breath.

Then one night, as the bats flitted for moths that
papered the sky like a child's cut-out stars, and the
bark of a fox was heard over the usual racket of owl
hoots, mosquito drones and the faint sound of breaking
waves, we reached the final page of Romy's manuscript.
Suddenly it was nearly over.

'It's the last one,' I said.

'Already?'

'Yes.'

'Are you sure?'

I held up the page. 'Quite sure.'

Dulcie poured us each an especially large brandy.
She adjusted herself in her chair and then cleared her
throat.

'Well, then. We have come this far – we must
proceed, at all costs.'

I looked at the page. 'I'm a little stuck on the title of this one. It's in German.'

'Read it, please.'

I broke the word down and read it slowly. '*Über-schwem-mungs-tod.*' I said it again. '*Überschwemmungs-tod.*'

Dulcie smiled. 'Bless the Germans. They have a word for everything and when they don't they craft a bastard hybrid on the spot. Many the mangled word has been grafted to another, Dr Frankenstein-like, and then reanimated into existence. This is one of them.'

'What does it mean?'

'*Überschwemmung* would suggest flooding or sub-mersion, or perhaps a deluge. And *Tod* is, of course, "death". So roughly translated it means "flooding death", or drowning.'

'Right.'

'It's Romy's little joke from beyond.'

I frowned.

'Oh, it's entirely in keeping with her humour, which was completely morbid and mordant too,' said Dulcie. 'I found it one of her most attractive qualities – that and her elusiveness. Because, you know, despite every-thing, I believe that Romy never fully revealed herself. Or at least not until her final act, anyway. Because there can be no greater revelation to the world than suicide, can there? It is the final ultimate outing of the cold inner truth of the tormented. The grandest gesture. A full stop forever.'

I realised then why Dulcie and Romy had gravitated to one another: it was becoming clear that they shared certain very similar character traits.

Dulcie sighed slowly and deeply.

'I just wish I could have said goodbye. Please read it now, Robert.'

I did.

Überschwemmungstod

And now the animals are braying in the burning stable
and scorched birds plummet from the sky.

You no longer stoop to lift the gasping fish,
stranded, beached on the gravel bank,

nor falter as a foam tide brings bubbling blood,
and shrieking shapes cross the ruined sun.

You are lost in the lie of your life now.
Perhaps you were only ever a rumour of a person –

a few good lines, scratched across the page like fresh scars.
A butterfly trapped in a childhood jam jar.

You are: wet kindling, green smoke, a dead jellyfish;
your mother's son and your father's daughter, all fiction.

So say farewell, then, in these dying days of April,
a thin string of hollow words your worthless legacy

as you drop the final mask and make your mark on the map
sealed beneath rotting boards, a self, all out at sea.

As I completed the final line, the colour drained from Dulcie's face. I found the poem horrific, and a little repetitive – the same repeated image of the grounded fish – and assumed she had felt the same.

'By Christ,' she said.

'What is it?'

'She's reaching out.'

'I don't quite understand.'

'Can't you see? She's reaching out. I knew she would eventually.'

'I'm afraid – '

She cut me off. 'Did you pull up any floorboards while working on the studio?'

'No,' I replied. 'But I fixed one or two that were loose.'

'More visibly loose than others?'

'I'm not sure. Perhaps.'

'Then you must show me where.'

'But why?'

'It's right there in the poem, Robert. Don't you see?'

I didn't.

'She's reaching out to me from her watery grave,' said Dulcie, a tremble of excitement in her voice. '"Sealed beneath rotting boards, a self, all out at sea." It's Romy's final farewell. I knew she would make contact in the end. I bloody knew it.'

X

In the shack I pushed my blankets and sleeping bag aside and pointed to the floorboards. 'Do you mean these?'

'Good lord,' she said. 'You can see just by looking. Fetch me a tool, will you.'

'Which one?'

'Any one, it doesn't matter.'

I found a chisel and before I could give it to her Dulcie snatched it from my hands and began hacking at the crack that separated the two boards. I handed her a hammer too. She threw her hat aside and strands of hair fell in her face as she wedged the bevelled blade of the chisel between the boards, levering first one and then the other, and then hitting it sternly and precisely with the hammer. The boards lifted. There was something frantic about her as she grabbed at the old wood, her hands slipping on their varnished surface and her nails scratching at the veneer. I had not seen her like this. She appeared in the grip of several conflicting emotions at once. Fury and urgency, perhaps. Panic. Excitement.

'Let me help you.'

She ignored me and with a sudden yanking motion wrenched the floorboards clean upwards with the reversed hammer head, the old nails squeaking as they slid from the old timber. Almost breathless now, she tossed the hammer aside, leaned forward and looked down.

And there it was: an envelope, placed in the secret space of the studio's cool stone foundations, just as she had predicted, laid there as the last act of a suicidal woman, a great poet, Dulcie Piper's soulmate. With a trembling hand she passed it to me. I took it.

Neither of us said anything for a moment. Then Dulcie urged me on.

'Well, open it, then.'

It suddenly felt heavy in my hand. Unduly weighted. Something unfamiliar and unwanted. Repellent, even.

'I'm not sure I can.'

'Just do it, will you.'

'But it's yours.'

'Open it.'

She hissed these words in such a manner that I could not refuse. I opened it.

'Read it.'

I began to read it.

'Out loud, Robert.'

So I did.

April 1st 1940

My dearest darling Honeyspinner,

If you have found this letter then you are as wonderful and clever and brilliant as I know you to be.

And if you have found this letter, then you have
also understood my work, and me. Well done. You
were the only one who came close – truly and always.

If you seek a reason, then it is this: I am
exhausted beyond belief. It is an eternal, malignant
exhaustion from which I know in my heart I can
never recover, for I carry deep within me a thousand
shadows that neither light nor laughter can possibly
reach. On this day for fools, all I want is to sleep
forever, so sleep I shall, beneath a blanket of water.
A fool I surely am, but I think of little else now.

The world is rotten to the core and soon all
will be war. My nation has wreaked unspeakable
havoc, and it will happen again and again. Other
nations, other dictators, will take the place of those
who have the whip hand now. They will have their
moment and soon war will become all that we
know, a constant state, until everything is razed. I
am certain that man will not make it to the twenty-
first century, and it's an unpardonable crime that he
will surely take woman with him.

This world I see emerging is no place for a
self-absorbed poet, especially one who has lost her

voice. I am rendered helpless, useless, meaningless. Of zero worth.

But you are strong, Dulcie Piper. The strongest there has ever been. A warrior queen. Know this: you will make it with or without me. I know you will.

I'm afraid I cannot atone for my premature departure. I just can't. But what I can apologise for is leaving you behind. You must know, my love, that it was only you who has made this existence tolerable these past years. Our time here would have been perfect were it not for my whirligig mind. I thank you for showing me this paradise, though we both know that in time paradise too becomes corrupted. It is already written.

I thank you, thank you, thank you for doing your best.

As I depart I bestow upon you my worthless work, an underweight and stillborn selection if ever there was. Stupid symbols in ink on paper – that's all they are. Nothing more. A void of sorts. Burn it, bin it, feed it to the useless docile chickens who seem so content in their idiocy; do with it what you will. It has first cursed and now finally defeated me.

With love, I will leave now.
Romy Landau

Beneath the letter there was another sheet of paper. On it were typed four lines. I read these too.

Fortified by laughter,
galvanised by love,

I am forever
in your atoms.

When I looked up, Dulcie was silently sobbing. Her face was a crumpled rag and her shoulders shook, as if her body was finally expelling the grief that had been held tightly within, slowly infecting her like a slow-releasing poison since that April day over six years ago. And now it had found an outlet.

Immobile, I held the letter by my side. I was not yet emotionally equipped to deal with such a situation. Instead I stood there in the sunlit studio, unmoving, as compassionate as a piece of furniture, and let Dulcie, who appeared to shrink in size as she sobbed, cry until the judders that racked her body gradually slowed to a halt.

When she stopped, she dabbed first one eye on her cuff and then the other, then looked around. When her eyes settled on one of my oily old rags, she heartily blew her nose into it three times. She arranged her hair, then replaced her hat, and a sense of complete calm seemed to wash over her. She appeared to stretch to full stature once more and it was as if she were emerging from a deep and satisfying sleep. Dulcie smiled.

'Well, now. I feel much better after that. Much better indeed. My pipes are cleared; I am a woman reborn.'

'I'm sorry, Dulcie. I'm sorry about Romy and the letter and everything.'

'*Sorry?* I'm not crying because I'm distraught, I'm crying for beauty and poetry and the brilliant last act of a unique mind. I'm crying because I knew she wouldn't let me down. Not really.'

She closed her eyes and recited the lines she had heard only once: '"Fortified by laughter, / galvanised by love, / I am forever / in your atoms."' Perfect. Just perfect.'

She opened her eyes again.

'I think perhaps you were right all along, Robert.'

'About what?'

'About *The Offing*.'

'In what way?'

'What was it you said? That you thought the book was brilliant and that other people might feel the same? So simple, and so true. You spoke from the heart, and the heart must always be listened to. Perhaps the world is ready for Romy's final work.'

'Or perhaps you are ready too?' I offered.

'Yes,' she said quietly. 'That also.'

'Do you mean you'll get it published?'

'I'll try my damnedest – with your help.'

'But I don't know anything about poetry or the book world.'

'You know more than you did, and you're too involved to wriggle out now. You've done the vital part: you have brought the book – and me – back into being. We are two midwives together, and we must ensure a safe birth into the world. Don't worry: I shall take care of the particulars.'

I smiled. 'That's wonderful, Dulcie.'

'There's just one thing – I should wish to hold back this one poem.'

She took the page from me and studied it for a moment.

'This one is for me and me alone. Perhaps it is selfish, but I must keep something of Romy back for myself. And you must keep these four lines a secret inside you forever. Hold them there.'

And I have – until now.

Something changed in the air that night. I awoke to dribbles of condensation glistening on the window and the sight of my breath billowing from beneath my blankets with each yawning exhalation.

The breeze had changed direction and the air had an edge to it now. It was bladed. It tasted damp and nutty. We were approaching the turning season of smoke and decay, of nest-building and leaves curling. The time of plenty promised by a summer that had seemed endless in its infancy was now drawing to a close, as it always does, yet it had somehow, for a while at least, managed to trick my mind into thinking that the outcome might possibly be different. Just as comfort and complacency were in danger of becoming a habit, and a pervasive sense of pleasurable slothfulness had begun to define each day, the lifting winds now brought autumn's advance party. We had entered the dying days.

The animal kingdom was already beginning its preparations.

The studio was cold. I burrowed deep below my blankets and hugged my knees to my chest. The first sighted robin landed on the cabin's windowsill and cocked a curious head at me.

The meadow seemed altered too, less alive with the violence of life, and more settled. It appeared bedded in, and a little maudlin, yet accepting of its fate and ready for the autumnal rot. It was quite ready for the incoming season of death in a way that I was not. Acting on the instinct of successive generations, the birds were busy.

In my naivety I had not once fully entertained the notion that my stay at the shack in the meadow by the cottage above the bay in this glorious green corner of Yorkshire would come to an end. It had only ever been there as a brief shadow-thought in the back of my gladly distracted mind, yet now for the first time in my sixteen short years I found myself asking: where does life go?

I rolled up my sleeping bag and blankets and tied them with twine into a tight bundle, then made a neat stack of the books that Dulcie had lent me, proud to have ploughed through them as a farmer stoically ploughs a field thick with rocks, roots and boulders, content in the knowledge that from his dogged toil great things might grow.

The briefcase of typed poems sat on the windowsill. I looked out across the meadow one final time, to the distant sea, to the offing, where Romy's remains were, and meditated on the idea that those words of hers that lay before me now might soon be available to the entire world.

And soon too would this place – this procreant, teeming Eden – be a secret no more, and instead be the subject of deep analysis and study, pilgrimage and memorial.

Soon *The Offing* would be beyond the horizon, and out there in the wide unknown.

———————

It was too chilly to breakfast outside so we ate a simple meal of toast and jam in Dulcie's front room.

Rendered impotent, the nettles were dying in small cemetery plots of benign brown clusters. I pointed to them. 'What will you do now?' I asked.

'I thought I might investigate an alternative. Mint seems the obvious choice, though I'm not sure why I've only just thought of it now. Or perhaps dandelion root. It'll be fun to find out what works and what doesn't. I mean, how bad can any of them be?'

I laughed. 'Pretty bad, I'd say.'

We sat in silence for there was little else to say. Without speaking a word, we both knew that it was time to leave.

Even Butler seemed to detect my imminent departure. Ever the sentinel, he sat beside me and every now and again touched my wrist – a wrist that weeks earlier he had coveted as a chewy snack – with his cold, wet nose.

I cleared the cups and plates and then when there was nothing left to do I stood awkwardly in the doorway for a moment. I moved from one foot to the other.

'Thank you for letting me stay. You've taught me so much.'

'Nonsense,' said Dulcie, turning away and lifting the cups and plates from the sink and back onto the table. Her eyes would not meet mine. 'If anything, I've held you captive.'

I moved some dirty pans into the sink, but Dulcie lifted those out too. I remembered her maxim about washing-up.

'That's not true. All the stories you've told and the food you've cooked for me. And the books too. I mean, I don't understand quite a bit of what I've read, but I've enjoyed it. And I feel especially lucky to have been able to read Romy's writing. I wouldn't have experienced any of this if I hadn't met you.'

Dulcie left the kitchen and went into the parlour. 'No,' she said from the other room, her voice raised too loud. 'You would have learned other things through other people instead. Other experiences. But I'm not so ungracious as to reject a heartfelt compliment. Just be aware that anything you've learned, you have learned yourself. All I've done is point you towards it.'

When I went into the living room to see what she was doing, Dulcie was standing at the window, looking out across the meadow. She was avoiding me.

'I think you're being modest,' I said quietly.

'I may be many things,' she said, with her back still turned to me, 'but modest is not one of them. Besides, it's a two-way street: you've more than earned your keep fixing this place up. Without you the meadow would have eaten me up soon enough and – ' Dulcie paused. 'Well. Let's just say that you've done more than you can ever know, for you have brought more than one person back to life.'

She finally turned to me and saw me blushing. She looked away again. At the carpet, at the pictures – at Romy – hanging on the wall. And then back to the window.

'It's true. Turn yourself into a beetroot if you want, but you have contributed to literary history, Robert.'

'What will happen to the poems now?'

'Tomorrow I shall go to Whitby and have copies made, and then I shall send them by special overnight delivery to Romy's editor, who writes twice a year to politely request whether I might have about my person any of those unpublished works which are the subject of much rumour and speculation. I've always ignored him until now – let the fucker salivate a while, that has always been my opinion. But I do believe now is the time. I should imagine we will then broker a nice little deal that will keep everyone happy. Of course, it's not about the money, but does fifty-fifty on the royalties suit?'

'*Suit?*'

Dulcie said all of this to a view of the meadow, but finally she turned around and her eyes fixed on mine for the first time during the conversation.

'Yes. Are you content with fifty per cent? Before you protest, let me first point out that poetry sells about as well as iron eagle insignias in Stamford Hill. That is to say, most don't care for it, and it might equate to half of bugger all. But, still. I happen to think these works are priceless and I am giving you a share of that, whether you like it or not. I'll even throw in as much honey as you can eat.'

'In that case,' I beamed, not fully appreciating the import of this casual offer in which Dulcie was effectively lining me up as sole beneficiary and executor, 'I accept.'

'Whatever happens, just make sure you *live*, Robert. Go out there. See Europe at the very least while you can, because soon enough someone else will decide to try to destroy it again. And, God knows, they like to rope the young into their messes.'

We stood like this for a moment longer and then I picked up my pack and turned and left the cottage, then walked down the lane that led to the future, the cooling sun at my back.

I did not go any further south.

Instead I turned north again, back towards the only place I knew.

It was harvest time and as I walked I saw the summer's end in all its golden glory.

I passed fields busy with men and women raking grass and hay into windrows, or stacking sheaves and building ricks of hay on carts. I saw work parties breaking for lunches of bread and cheese and raw onions eaten like apples, and often I stopped and asked if they needed help, and was given a day or two here and there, and this time around I was stronger, fitter and possessed by a greater stamina, and I was fed well for my troubles too. My appetite appeared greater than ever, yet each night I still fell asleep in barns and sheepfolds and haystacks with my stomach growling.

I saw orchards of trees hanging heavy with apples that would soon be ripe for plucking, the bounty going into pies or paper twists for winter, or to the press for cider that was often made communally in villages. I saw the slow turning of the season, a charring at the edges of everything. Mornings damp with dew took longer to dry out and the insects seemed fewer, and sluggish too. I felt a stiffness in my knees, ankles and hips and my boots were in dire need of new soles. One was laced with a piece of baling twine.

The breeze that blew inland carried with it new scents. Woodsmoke, earth, fruit in fullness. Many of the brambles were laden with blackberries that were already rotten, the beautiful jewels of summer now lacking lustre and mushy to the touch, gorged upon by drowsy wasps drunk on the first stages of fermentation. The finest gossamer webs were strung across their tangled vines; they belonged to the spiders now, though one evening I unexpectedly chanced upon a wild strawberry patch and was glad to fill myself with what was surely the last batch of the year. Soon the morning frosts would see them done for. I spent that night picking seeds from my teeth, and in the morning I stood and stretched and walked on.

And then one day the towers of the cathedral emerged before me, a stone citadel poking up through the canopy of trees to pierce the firmament and lift the souls of those who gazed upon it, and I knew that I was only a brisk day's walk from home.

As I walked through the village I was barely recognised. My black hair, shorn short in the spring, was now thick and hung in salt-tangled ringlets, my skin was the colour of the honey that Dulcie would soon be spinning down in the meadow, and I had filled out so that my clothes appeared to belong to a smaller man slight in stature. I nodded at acquaintances and more than once was met with the narrowed eyes of suspicion reserved for strangers who entered this odd and isolated little world of the colliery that was still war-racked, as all such places were, but nevertheless remained devoted to the excavation of the prized anthracite from the deep and ancient land.

In September I went to the pit. Yet instead of being handed a lamp and hard hat, my father, perhaps recognising that I wasn't suited to a life at the seam, and wanting me to have a position safer than the one he had held working the coalface for four decades, had somehow wangled an apprenticeship in the office above ground. I had done well in my examinations – better, perhaps, than anyone had expected of this young daydreamer – but it was a coveted position that rarely became vacant, and even then it was usually awarded to the pit manager's son or daughter, who might hold it for years. Decades, even.

I was supposed to be grateful. A clerical position was a safe position in all respects, but especially the important one: no one ever got crushed beneath a collapsing pile of paperwork or blown to smithereens drinking tea and filing payslips in the comfort and warmth of an office on a cold North-East winter's day.

But no one ever found adventure in ledger books and dockets either. The concept of a job for a life was too horrific to consider, and every time I was forced to do just that, or saw the look of pride on my mam's face as I sat down to tea each night, I was sent into a sort of deep existential panic akin to that, I imagine, experienced by someone who has been handed a full-term life sentence in chokey.

How could I sit indoors, when all that life was out there, being lived by others?

I stuck it out and saved what I could, each day eating my way through the bland contents of my bait box, and then stepping out into the cold air with the siren's wail each evening. Autumn drew in, and the leaves fell, and each evening I went for a walk around the lanes and fields surrounding the village, but now the lanes appeared drab and the rutted fields flat, barren and purely functional. I would return home with my breath before me and my boots heavy with clods of blackened mud, and retire to my room with a poetry book.

I had begun to take them out of the local library, and had soon worked my way through the narrow collection there, so I took to ordering other titles in. I had a taste for it now and the librarian was more than happy to oblige me.

One Sunday I walked the several miles to the sea, but was saddened to find it a grey wash, a broth of brine and coke dust, the beach too a gritted, blackened bank of coal containing the occasional limb of stripped bone-white driftwood, where even the shriek of the seagulls sounded like warning shots to ward off strangers.

I suffered a lot of headaches caused by the dim light in the pit office and from all the reading I did at night in bed, hunched beneath the covers with a torch.

Then it was winter. It came in on an easterly wind and was the coldest for decades. Snow fell and kept falling and for a few days the light was brilliant and the village sang with the excited chatter of children, but temperatures kept falling and soon everything stiffened, then became solid. The soil, the hot-water pipes.

The snowdrifts grew deeper and out on the uplands entire flocks of sheep perished beneath a great ocean of whiteness, their corpses dug out and heaped in stiff piles. Supplies could not get through and the village became cut off; our ration-book basics were being stretched and some days we lived off tea and flour pancakes. Cows began to starve in their barns, and chickens too, thousands upon thousands of them in poultry farms. Even the pits closed and very quickly there was not enough coal to fuel the power stations. It was as if the war had not ended at all, and had in fact got worse, and the government was in disarray, and we all faced the festive season with empty cupboards.

Snow silenced us.

At home I shovelled snow and looked in on elderly neighbours but otherwise stayed as close to the fire as I could, drinking tea, reading, and now and again writing a few rudimentary lines of poetry. There was nothing else to be done but wait the winter out and hope for better days.

I thought of Dulcie often, and Romy too, and when the snow finally began to melt and the pit reopened I tramped my way back to work, wondering if this was adulthood, and whether this was my life, my world, forever.

One day when the last of the snow was melting away and the supply lines were open once again, my mother took delivery of a large crate.

When she lifted the lid she was surprised to see a fat goose staring back at her. She led me to it in the backyard when I got home from work and pointed. The bird did not seem unduly perturbed by its new surroundings.

Taped to the inside of the crate was a flat parcel bound by many, many sheets of greaseproof paper. It was addressed to me.

As I unwrapped it, an envelope fell out from between the layers. Though Christmas had long been and gone, it contained a festive card in which the following message was written in large untamed handwriting:

Belatedly
to you and yours,
from me and mine.

I continued to unwrap the parcel and when the final piece fell away I held a thin, ornately bound hardback book with an embossed cover. I turned it over in my hand and admired the spine and then the endpapers. It was a marvel to behold.

As I opened it my heart appeared to quicken. There, facing the title page, was a frontispiece that depicted on it a finely detailed illustration of Dulcie's studio as it had surely looked when it was first occupied. Around it was the meadow, and in the far distance, rendered accurately and beautifully, was the bay and the sea. There was even a dog lolling in the long grass. It was Butler.

I turned the page and read the words:

The Offing
by Romy Landau

And then below that, written in a smaller font:

Edited
by Dulcie Piper & Robert Appleyard

I couldn't believe it. I turned the pages, quickly flipping past the contents page and through the collection that little over half a year earlier had been a file of neglected paper gathering dust in a building in danger of being slowly consumed by the landscape and the elements.

As the crisp, freshly cut leaves of paper fluttered between my fingers, lines from the poems jumped out at me now like familiar friends returning, and when I turned back to the title page and read my name once more I realised I was holding my breath.

She had done it. Dulcie Piper had done it. *The Offing* had arrived. She had found a publisher and not only was the book one of the most beautiful things I had ever seen, but my name was in it.

I looked at my mother and then at the goose, and both of them looked back at me.

And I smiled.

The land was greening again, but was not yet so fulsome as the tangled corridor that I had left during the dying days of summer past.

I had lasted seven months as an apprenticed clerk at the colliery and confirmed member of a trade union. Even with many days off during the cold, cruel winter, it was a gestation period more than long enough to birth in me a stifling sense of claustrophobia and a distrust of authority that endures to this day.

I had quickly learned that if I didn't act otherwise I would be in that drab office for life, and if witnessing a war, even from afar, like some sort of strange game played by adults that got out of hand, had taught me one thing it was that life is short, and we each only have one shot at it, so as Easter approached – and against the pleas of my parents, who did little to disguise their disappointment, and despite the potential ostracism from those in the village who thought it a personal insult that I should walk away from a position of far greater privilege than those who risked their lives several hundred feet underground – I handed in my resignation. At the age of seventeen I had retired from servitude.

My timing was good. Just two months earlier a notice had gone up at the gates announcing that the entire British coal industry was to be nationalised in order to address what the government called the 'idleness' that pervaded in those shattered days of recuperation that followed the war. The harsh Baltic winter had scared the industry too, and now the newly formed National Coal Board would oversee the management of all the pits.

The long-held certainty that there would always be coal – and consequently there would always be work mining it – was the foundation of my village. But some of us saw that changing. Though money was still being invested in new sinkings and the mechanisation of the transportation of coal overground, the final chapter was already being written. The industry was contracting. It would be a long, slow death.

And I was glad to have got out.

———

An unexpected nervousness coursed through me as the lane dropped down into a shaded hollow and then there it was, Dulcie's cottage, and a moment later there too was Butler, panting as he padded out to meet me in his quiet, graceful manner, to which I responded by squatting and giving him a big hug, and then feeding him the last of my three-day-old biscuits.

And then there too was Dulcie Piper, in her garden, just as I had left her. She was pruning plants.

'Ah,' she said. 'There you are. I suppose I should put the kettle on. Rosehip alright?'

'Rosehip?'

'Yes, for tea. I know what you're thinking: how has the old trout got rosehips when everyone knows they're strictly an autumnal and wintering fruit, but – '

Winking conspiratorially, she tapped the side of her nose.

'I was rather looking forward to some of your nettle tea,' I replied.

She made to spit. 'Ugh, vile stuff.'

'But I thought you loved it.'

'Did I? Well, I'm afraid you'll have to pick your own if you want some.'

'It's nice to see you, Dulcie. It's nice to be back again.'

'It's nice to see you too, Robert. And it's nice to have you back again. Butler will be glad of the company, I'm sure.'

The meadow was teeming once again, all my previous work cutting and unrooting undone by seeds and sun alone. It had come through one of the coldest winters on record and was approaching untamed wildness once more.

Only then did I see that the tangle of trees and weeds at the low end that once obscured the sea had been drastically pared back so that we could now enjoy a clear view all the way out across the bay and the water beyond it.

Dulcie saw me admiring the new, unhindered prospect.

'I thought it was finally time to forgive the tempest of the briny deep,' she said.

We drank our tea looking out across it as I summarised my short-lived career as a junior clerk, my recent resignation and my new regimen of reading. It felt as if only a day or two had passed, rather than a moribund autumn and that the prolonged winter of discontent had been a kick in the teeth to those hoping the aftermath of war might offer an easier life.

I talked for a long time and Dulcie listened without saying a word.

'It sounds to me as if you have done awfully well to dodge a bullet, Robert,' she said when I finally stopped. 'Very well indeed. Work is vastly overrated. Obviously some jobs are vital, but so many spend their limited time in this life devoted to drudgery. Me, I always chose pleasure at all costs. And anyway, listen to you.'

'What do you mean?'

'Last summer it took nigh on a week to get a peep out of you, and now the tap is on the water doth flow. Verbally speaking, I mean. What I'm saying is, you've grown into yourself. You'll linger longer, I hope?'

'I'd very much like to.'

'Good, because there's something I would like to show you.'

Butler led the way through the thicket to the studio. It too appeared much as I had left it, apart from one small thing: attached to the door was a large wooden plaque into which was engraved the letter 'R'.

'You named it after Romy,' I said.

Dulcie handed me a key. 'And you.'

I was confused. 'Me?'

'Of course. Here – ' She pressed the key into my palm and urged me to use it.

I slipped it into a new lock, opened the door and stepped into a fully furnished room. The place had been transformed with the addition of a wrought-iron bed, a small drop-leaf table, standard lamp, rugs, oil paintings and a fitted shelf that ran right around the cabin's interior above head height, and which held hundreds of books. On the table was a large black typewriter.

The wood burner was still in place but had been cleaned and restored, and next to it was a two-ring hotplate on a unit that held utensils, pans, plates, cutlery and so forth. A cupboard above held some basic provisions, and lined up on the windowsill were six large jars of dark honey that appeared near-iridescent as the sun shone through them to illuminate the tiny bubbles of air trapped within.

'Well?'

I was lost for words – almost.

'Did you do all of this?'

'I had to have a project over the winter. Besides, you had already done the lion's share. All I did was apply a bit of interior flair. It's yours.'

'Mine?'

'To stay in whenever you like. That way, whatever you do in life, or wherever you care to wander, you will always have a home here. I've written it into the deeds of the house. The studio is in your name now. The cottage may crumble and my bones may rot in the dank soil of deepest England, but you will always be able to stay here should you wish.'

'I don't know what to say.'

'Say nothing.'

I looked around the room, and felt I could not imagine anywhere else I would ever want to be. But there was one question I had to ask.

'Am I your project too, Dulcie?'

'That sounds so crass, Robert.'

'But am I?'

'Helping those I feel inclined to help is what I do. Everyone could use a patron.'

'This place must have cost –'

'A drop in the ocean. The fact is, it cost me very little as I'm pleased to report *The Offing* is selling like cinder toffee on a bank holiday. You see, the timeless poetry of Romy Landau paid for the bits and pieces – the licensing and reproduction fees alone have proved substantial. But let's not be vulgar and talk too much about money. Let us talk instead about the abundant amber nectar that was, of course, a gift from those friends of ours whom you most boldly and bravely plucked from the branch. Remember?'

I picked up one of the jars of honey and held it to the light.

'Of course I remember. I don't know what to say, Dulcie,' I said again.

'A simple "thank you" will suffice.'

'Thank you.'

'You don't have to thank me.'

I smiled. 'I won't, then. I retract it.'

'You're hungry, I expect?'

I nodded.

'Good, because I've got a chicken in the oven for you. It's got half a pound of bacon across its back and the same amount of sage and sausage meat shoved up it. I hope you're hungry.'

'But how did you know I was coming?'

Dulcie shrugged. 'Because the sap is rising and the ambrosia scent of summer is on the breeze again. I knew you'd be back.'

'But today?'

She brushed my question off. 'One of these days.'

I wondered how many chickens had been roasted and fed to Butler over the past few weeks.

'The meadow is a bit of mess,' I said through a quiet belch of satisfaction. I threw a large greasy piece of chicken thigh to Butler, who snatched it from the air with delight in his dark Teutonic eyes.

'Yes, well, I only got as far as hacking at the branches blocking my view,' said Dulcie. 'It's not so easy doing that when you're an old crone, alone, and there's frost on the ground. And ageing is so *tedious*. Avoid it at all costs, I say.'

'You're not alone now, though.'

She smacked her lips.

'I'll have to pay you, of course.'

'For what?'

'The meadow work.'

I laughed. 'You know I don't need paying. You only have to ask.'

'Well, there is just one more thing that I nearly forgot, actually.'

She stood and walked into the house, and then returned. She pushed aside the dish that held the remains of the chicken and placed an envelope in front of me.

'Your share of *The Offing* so far.'

I opened it up and pulled out a cheque for four hundred pounds. It was more than my father made in a year.

'I can't believe it,' I said.

'Believe it. There'll be more to come, no doubt, once it's out in paperback in the autumn. The hardback notices have been very good, and it's already into its third print run. This is almost unheard of in contemporary poetry. There's nothing the literary world likes more than a narrative of triumph and tragedy – it doesn't really matter in which order – and, Christ, Romy certainly exemplified that. Now that the dust of that silly war has settled, they want something else to write about, you see, and what better story than that of a doomed Germanic poet who wrote like an angel, burned brightly and briefly, and then ended it all rather than live in a world half-destroyed by her own kin. Lost at sea, forever a mystery. That's how they see it, anyway, and I'm not much inclined to correct any inaccuracies otherwise. Let the myth grow, I say, and fuck them all.'

She raised her glass. I did the same. We clinked them together.

'Now, I wouldn't dream of telling you how you might wish to spend this windfall, just as I wouldn't tell a tramp not to spend the pennies I've given him on a nice bottle of vintage meths. However, might I at least plant one seed of an idea? An investment, if you will.'

'Of course,' I said.

'University.' She raised a hand. 'Now, hear me out. I remember what you said, clear as day: "People like me don't go to places like that." Robert, that ripped at my heart. The thought that you see yourself as some-how inferior to the toffs, tossers and bashers I grew up amongst is an unforgivable absurdity and, furthermore, one that must be addressed immediately. Nothing will change if it's not changed from the inside, by which I mean if you were to go to university, you would not only be refining what is already a keen mind, but shift-ing the intake towards your people too. I know it's only a small step: the barriers can't all be broken at once. Who knows, though, perhaps one day when you're a wild success you could repay the favour to someone equally as deserving.'

'I wouldn't know where to start.'

'I'll help you.'

'What if I don't have the correct qualifications?'

She shook her head. 'There are ways,' said Dulcie. 'Trust me, there are ways. Special dispensations. There are scholarships. Also I recently read that there is talk of changing the entire further education system, and that there will soon be a new type of qualification that one will take in order to go up to university. They're wiping the slate and levelling the playing field, if you'll indulge me a double cliché. We could speed you through those,

I'm sure. Approached with alacrity, a bright boy like you who has his eyes and ears open to experience can't fail to find a place somewhere. Believe in yourself, Robert, that's all it takes. Unless of course you don't want to.'

'No,' I said, 'I want to. At least I think I do.'

She stood up and picked up the plates.

'Mull it over while I fetch dessert. Take your time. You're on holiday. But do give it some thought.'

'I still don't understand why you're being so generous, Dulcie.'

'I told you, it's what I do. And maybe one day you will too.'

I lean back in my chair. My neck aches. The pain still throbs there, down one side, as it has for these past few months. I swallow painkillers like confectionery but they do little. I have bottles of pills but the one thing they cannot do is defeat death.

I remove my glasses, stand and stretch, then lean over to survey the words I have painstakingly typed, my wrists and knuckles aching. I am not as fast as I used to be. Old age has spun cobwebs in all my joints and the illness has slowed me right down in ways I could never have imagined, but at least my memory works. That muscle is still strong.

Though there is a chill in the air, the window is open wide and a stone from the beach keeps the pile of papers in place. The stone holds within it a fossil. An ammonite. To look at it makes me feel young again. All time is relative and on certain days when I am not moving and I close my eyes and tune in to nature's frequency, I am sixteen again.

Every now and then a gentle gust lifts the pages to afford a glimpse of a sentence that takes me straight back to those moments I have documented upon which my entire life pivoted, and then changed direction entirely.

Because really the story started long ago, here in this shack that sits sagging in a wild meadow now. Perhaps you read about it in newspaper profiles or the documentary they made about me following the publication of a debut novel that the critics said heralded an angry new voice, and which sold unexpectedly well. They were wrong: I wasn't angry. I just wrote what I knew. That was how I talked. That was how we all talked up north. And still do.

Time was on my side then. Youth had recently become a commodity to market and apparently I was one of the voices that captured it – a spokesperson for the young and disenfranchised, no less, they said. I just wrote what I saw and heard all around me, back in the village. I painted the people onto the page, that's all. Nothing more. That those in London considered my novel and the many more that followed it to be strange and exotic only showed how far removed they were from the true working heartlands of an England in a state of change. When it was adapted for film, that chasm only widened. But I happily accepted the accolades, and cashed the cheques, and I never forgot Dulcie.

How could I?

Each summer I returned, even when married with children, even after Dulcie Piper was long gone, first to a luxurious split-level apartment overlooking the grassy parklands of The Stray in Harrogate, followed by several years in a nursing home on the fringes of York, and then finally to a few fading days in hospital. I visited her in each; she was lucid and witty and caustic to the end. She passed away while wearing oversized sunglasses, full of gin.

Regimes rose and fell and I kept coming back here, to the meadow, to write and read and think, to take grass baths in the moonlight and watch badgers at dawn. Divorces and deaths and grandchildren occurred and still I returned, always alone, until the stays became so prolonged that I never left, and my big old house – up against this place I could never call it a home – sat empty.

With Dulcie at my shoulder the words kept flowing. I hear her always, prodding and cajoling my every clumsy sentence, urging me onwards to always do better. And so the books kept coming, admittedly to a dwindling readership, but they always made it to the shelf. And that is what matters. I was living the life I wanted to live, and still am, despite this thing that eats away inside of me: a disease called time.

The sea air is good for me too. It gives me an appetite, and when one has an appetite the will to live is strong.

Dulcie is here now, in the room, standing behind me, uncorking a bottle as she looks out across to the meadow to the sea, to the offing, and the sun that sets behind it. Sometimes I walk up to the little graveyard and sit by her headstone, amongst those of the sailors and fishermen, and I know that soon enough I will lie down and join them. Perhaps we shall share our stories.

That way of life has changed, of course. The small-scale fishing industry barely exists and most of the houses down bay are second homes that fill up only during holidays. It doesn't bother me. The rest of the year I get the beach to myself. I walked along it early this morning, and saw how much the coast had eroded since I enjoyed that first view of it. The sea has eaten away at it so that the country has shrunk by twenty or thirty feet just in my lifetime, and it will keep shrinking. It will diminish to a pebble, and then one day nothing, as we all do. It is a reminder that permanence is an impossibility. All is flux. And nature always wins.

I sit back down and type the final sentence of the story about lives led as freely as greater forces would permit.

These are my last words, and I leave them here for you.

Acknowledgements

With thanks gratitude to my agent, Jessica Woollard, and everyone at David Higham Associates: Alice Howe, Clare Israel and Penelope Killick. Thanks to my editor, Alexa von Hirschberg, who helped shape and refine this book, always with the lightest of touches. To all at Bloomsbury: Ros Ellis, Marigold Atkey, Philippa Cotton, Rachel Wilkie, Jasmine Horsey. Thank you also to Silvia Crompton for the copyediting, and Zaffar Kunial for his poetry input.

Writers rely on luck, and I have had a generous share. For their support and encouragement over the years I also wish to acknowledge Claire Malcolm and all at New Writing North. Kevin and Hetha Duffy at Bluemoose Books. Carol Gorner and everyone at the Gordon Burn Trust. Richard and Elizabeth Buccleuch and the Walter Scott Prize. Michael Curran at Tangerine Press. Jeff Barrett and all at Caught by the River. Sarah Crown and Arts Council England. The Society of Authors. The Royal Society of Literature. The Northern Fiction Alliance.

To my family and friends, and my wife, Adelle Stripe.

The bulk of *The Offing* was written in libraries by hand, using pen and paper. This book is dedicated to librarians everywhere, and to booksellers and teachers, and all who work towards sharing a passion for the power of the written word.

Note on the Author

Benjamin Myers was born in Durham in 1976. His novel *The Gallows Pole* received a Roger Deakin Award and won the Walter Scott Prize for historical fiction. *Beastings* won the Portico Prize for Literature and *Pig Iron* won the Gordon Burn Prize, while *Richard* was a *Sunday Times* Book of the Year. He has also published poetry, crime novels, short fiction and the nature memoir *Under the Rock*, while his journalism has appeared in publications including, among others, the *Guardian*, *New Statesman*, *Caught by the River* and the *Spectator*.

He lives in the Upper Calder Valley, West Yorkshire.

Note on the Type

The text of this book is set Adobe Garamond. It is one of several versions of Garamond based on the designs of Claude Garamond. It is thought that Garamond based his font on Bembo, cut in 1495 by Francesco Griffo in collaboration with the Italian printer Aldus Manutius. Garamond types were first used in books printed in Paris around 1532. Many of the present-day versions of this type are based on the *Typi Academiae* of Jean Jannon cut in Sedan in 1615.

Claude Garamond was born in Paris in 1480. He learned how to cut type from his father and by the age of fifteen he was able to fashion steel punches the size of a pica with great precision. At the age of sixty he was commissioned by King Francis I to design a Greek alphabet, and for this he was given the honourable title of royal type founder. He died in 1561.